I0739440

THE Real Thing

SUSANN ORIEL

CRIMSON
ROMANCE

F+W Media, Inc.

Copyright © 2014 by Susann Oriel.

All rights reserved.
This book, or parts thereof, may not be reproduced in any form without permission from the publisher; exceptions are made for brief excerpts used in published reviews.

Published by
Crimson Romance
an imprint of F+W Media, Inc.
10151 Carver Road, Suite 200
Blue Ash, OH 45242. U.S.A.
www.crimsonromance.com

ISBN 10: 1-4405-8554-7
ISBN 13: 978-1-4405-8554-8
eISBN 10: 1-4405-8555-5
eISBN 13: 978-1-4405-8555-5

This is a work of fiction. Names, characters, corporations, institutions, organizations, events, or locales in this novel are either the product of the author's imagination or, if real, used fictitiously. The resemblance of any character to actual persons (living or dead) is entirely coincidental.

Cover art © 123RF/Andrey Kiselev

CHAPTER ONE

Gemma didn't know which was worse, a million goose bumps or old Mr. Rainey.

"Ladies and gentlemen, we start the bidding at $10 million."

The most important day of her young life, and McCallister's head auctioneer for the New York branch might as well be selling a paint-by-numbers kit. Why couldn't the man sound more enthusiastic? After all, this was a K. L. Wentworth watercolor up for sale—a multimillion-dollar work of art that she, clever Gemma Gilmore, had authenticated as genuine.

She should have stayed away from today's auction. It was too much, especially now that Mr. Rainey appeared to be doubly bored by a phone bid. "We have a bid for $11 million. Do I hear $11.1?"

Okay, enough of that dry, old stick. Just concentrate on who's bidding.

Snuggling herself back into the small alcove away from the crowd, Gemma scanned the spectators seated in neat rows across the auction room. Two of McCallister's regular bidders were in their usual row, ten seats apart. One was scratching his nose to place his bid, while the other bobbed his head to keep up. The entire auction room knew who they were. With those two well-known rival collectors of American twentieth-century paintings in attendance, everyone at McCallister's usually had a friendly bet on who would win. Gemma had already put her money on the Nose Scratcher taking home the Wentworth.

By the time she'd completed her room check, the bidding had picked up pace. "Ladies and gentlemen, I have a phone bid of $14 million."

Leaning forward out of the alcove, she scanned the back of the auction room thick with spectators, security guards, and every employee of the New York office. The whole staff usually turned out when the big works came up for sale. Gemma spotted her new appraisal intern looking in her direction. She smiled. He waved back.

The auctioneer stopped mid-drone. "James O'Mara, no bidding gestures—you know that."

Oh Lord, he's in for it now. Everyone turned to look toward the back wall. Laughter rippled across the room as Jamie uttered a bashful "sorry" before putting his head down. The poor guy had just broken the golden rule of auctions, and it was her fault.

"Ladies and gentleman," Mr. Rainey continued dryly, "now that young Jamie has decided not to bid for the Wentworth, the offer stands at $14 million." She sighed as chuckles flooded the room again. She'd have to buy Jamie a cheer-up drink after work.

Idly sweeping her gaze past Jamie, she studied the rest of the crowd. As usual, there were more people than seats, but those standing were only here for the ride and would probably drift off after the next big-item lot had sold. No eye-popping bids were likely to come from them. In fact, there was nobody interesting at all.

Oh, except for one. She would have missed him if it weren't for his impressive height. He stood in the far corner, half-obscured by a pillar and so well separated from the crowd, she briefly wondered why. He was far too broad-shouldered to be a typical art collector. True, they came in all shapes and sizes, but she could usually spot a collector at fifty yards, and they definitely didn't look like this guy. Under that dark business suit there was a powerful physique, and it hadn't gotten that way by hanging around auction rooms. A professional athlete, maybe? No, that wasn't it. Despite that easy stance, there was a strength and control way beyond athletic prowess. The man seemed almost ... *dangerous*.

Challenging.

She knew she shouldn't stare, but then again, why not? He was just one big aphrodisiac-on-a-stick. And the fact that she could drool over him from the safety of her alcove made it so much more delicious. Almost naughty.

Gemma stared harder when he brought a large, tanned hand up to rub along the dark stubble of his jaw. No wedding ring. Not that it meant anything of course, but still, the knowledge seemed to sweeten the view.

And what a view it was. Gemma actually licked at her lip when he shifted his weight and his jacket slipped open so she could savor the promise of rock-hard abs under the white business shirt. She shivered, her stomach doing somersaults at the thought of having those abs under her fingers. Under her mouth.

Oh mercy, she was an idiot. Her engagement might have ended two months ago, and of course she needed to get back in the swim, but ogling to the point of sexual fantasy was straight-out tragic. Besides, it was also a complete waste of time since she was one of those types who looked but never touched. That was her trouble. And she hadn't even done much of that lately, being too preoccupied with her job to look at anything other than paintings and her laptop. But then, she'd never seen a man like this at a McCallister's auction. Or anywhere else, for that matter.

"The bid is $15,900,000, ladies and gentlemen. This is your opportunity to own one of the great American watercolors. Do I hear $16 million?"

Gemma started when she heard the magic figure called out. The two most expensive paintings she'd ever authenticated were up for sale today, and the first one was close to setting the record for a Wentworth.

So she really should focus on the auction, but all she could do was stare at that corner. *But hell, that man is more beautiful than a hundred Wentworths.* A sexy Greek god, that's who he could be. Maybe Perses, the Titan god of destruction? He looked as if he could handle anything. Her, for instance. Right now.

Gemma chewed off the last of her lip gloss as Perses stepped forward from the pillar and slid his hands in his pockets, the movement stretching his suit pants temptingly across his crotch. Oh, but she just *had* to take a wee peek at that. Fantasize a little more. If that guy knew what was flipping around in her head, he'd have her arrested for mental molestation.

Was that the top of a tattoo peeking above his shirt collar? Lord, she so needed to know.

But how?

Perhaps she could step out of her alcove and catch his attention with a smile when he looked her way. The trouble was, he seemed to be more interested in the Wentworth than the crowd, so that probably wouldn't work. No, the only way to meet him was to go over there and start a conversation.

He was well away from the crowd and the auctioneer, so she wouldn't be disturbing anybody. And there was no reason why she couldn't watch the rest of the auction with Perses. It was totally appropriate. After all, this was a prestigious auction house, not a bar. Besides, if he didn't want company, she could simply say she had mistaken him for someone else. Or something like that.

The sharp bang of Mr. Rainey's gavel snapped her attention back to the auction. "Sold, to Number 214 on the floor for $17 million." The Nose Scratcher had come in with a final, devastating bid. Wow. A record. No one had expected the Wentworth to do so well, considering most of the artist's other works had dropped in value over the past five years. Today's record sale would automatically add hundreds of thousands in value to every other Wentworth. And she had played a key part. Her day was shining brighter by the minute.

"Ladies and gentlemen, there will be a short break while the next lot is prepared."

Perfect timing. Gemma tucked a stray curl behind an ear, straightened her black mini dress, and, in a moment of pure recklessness, undid two buttons of the bodice, then did them up again. Way too obvious. Besides, with her good legs and new five-inch pumps, she didn't need the extra help from her cleavage.

But what would she actually *do* if she gained his interest? Ask him out?

Sure, why not?

You can do this, Gemma.

Armed with her brand-new confidence, she slipped out the nearest exit door and walked quickly along the passage to the side door closest to Perses. He didn't seem to notice her when she stepped in quietly. Or had he? Side-on to her, he was staring straight ahead, but Gemma had the impression by the way he shifted on his feet that he'd put her in his peripheral vision. That he was studying her. His hands were still in his pockets, stretching the fabric ...

Whatever you do, don't look down!

Gemma breathed in deep and coughed. "Excuse me."

He didn't turn. "Yeah."

Not a good start. "I was wondering if you ... " Hell, this was all wrong. The man obviously wasn't up for company. Okay, it was time to execute the backup plan. "I'm sorry, I thought you were someone else."

She'd only just rotated on a heel to hightail it back to her alcove when the deep voice cemented her to the spot.

"Who?"

Who? Good question. "Um ... just someone ... you wouldn't know him."

"Maybe I would," the voice insisted quietly. "Who?"

She turned, knowing her whole body, right down to her toes, was turning pink with embarrassment—and she was helpless to prevent it.

"No, really, you wouldn't know him," she squeaked, wondering if making a run for it would look too undignified.

Too late. He'd already turned and taken a casual, yet somehow controlled, step toward her. A pair of dark hazel eyes locked on hers. Eyes that might pass for a deep auburn in the sun. Irises flecked with black. Utterly charismatic.

"Why have you been staring at me?"

"Sorry?"

"Don't play dumb."

Heat flared at the insult. Fine eyes or not, the man was flat-out rude. But then, her half-baked idea to introduce herself to the sexiest man she'd ever laid eyes on was turning into one of her all-too-frequent silly decisions when it came to men. She'd never been very good at impromptu introductions, especially to the hot ones, and what a moment to remind herself of the fact.

"As I—I explained," she stammered, furious with herself as much as at him, "I thought you were someone else."

His brow rose in surprise, drawing her attention to his features. An outdoors face, rugged and tanned. Undeniably good-looking, especially with that hard-cut profile and masculine mouth so full of sensual promise. Of course, he had to know it. A hundred women would have given him a heads-up on that. Yet somehow he didn't seem the type who spent a lot of time doing the dating thing.

"Right. And it took you ten minutes of staring and unbuttoning your dress to come over and talk to this 'someone else.' Lucky guy," he said without a trace of humor. "What were you intending to offer him?"

World, stop and let me off. The man had seen everything. Her eyes flew down to check her buttons, knowing his gaze was right behind hers. Thank God, still together. He had to think her an idiot for sure. And if she had any doubt about it, his dry tone confirmed it.

"I'm impressed with your"—he flicked a less-than-subtle glance down at her legs—"*resourcefulness.* So how do you know this lookalike?"

Now he wanted *details*?

"We dated for a short time," she blurted out. Surely that would shut him up long enough for her to escape. "Anyway, I have to go."

"I'm afraid you can't go."

Of course she could go. Who on earth did this guy think he was, ordering her around on her territory? "Says who?" she argued. Sexy Greek god or not, she was so done with this conversation. "Who do you think—"

"The auction is about to start again. You'll have to stay here ... with *me*." It was quietly said but with enough authority to clamp her mouth shut. But dammit, he was right. If she left the auction room, she wouldn't be allowed back in. It was one of McCallister's rules that no one, not even an employee, could break when the big works were up for sale.

While she dithered for an answer, he smiled and looked her over again. "I can see you're okay with that?"

Lord, if this wasn't a mess. Her brain was urging her to make an exit, her idiot body arguing the point. Besides, the next lot was her main reason for being in the auction room today, and to leave because of Perses, or whoever he was, was ridiculous.

But where to stand? The pillar. "This will do," she breathed, taking the few steps to reach it, ready to hug the thing for support.

He seemed pleased with her decision. "Good. I'll stand with you." His deep voice drowned her senses like some rich Kentucky bourbon. That voice alone was a lethal drug.

When he moved to within inches of her back, Gemma realized with a sick thud that she'd put herself exactly where he wanted her. She was trapped between the pillar and Perses.

Gemma shifted on her feet, her whole body tingling with awareness that his chin was only inches from the top of her head. Too close. Too tall. Even in heels, she barely reached past his collar ...

Collar? She'd not checked out his tattoo, but it hardly mattered now. The most expensive work she'd ever authenticated was up for sale, and this was her big day.

"Lot 59. *Dreaming Atlantis* by Frank Bonvalet. Oil on canvas, 1912. Known as the 'lost work' when it disappeared forty years ago after a prolonged ownership dispute. For the first time ever, Bonvalet's most elusive work is up for sale. We have an opening phone bid of $25 million."

The crowd gasped in unison. A high opening bid, but the work was expected to sell for around $35 million.

The bourbon voice rumbled down at her. "You like the Bonvalet?"

"Sorry?" Gemma muttered inanely. Then, when he waited in silence, she added on a rush, "Oh, yes, I do like it."

"What do you like about it?"

"Um ... " She groped for something to say. She couldn't think with that big body perilously close. "I ... I guess it's the way Bonvalet uses color and light, especially where the land meets the sea. It's like one cannot exist without the other. Like ... " She paused, wondering if she should dare risk using the word "lovers."

"Lovers?" He echoed the word so softly she could barely hear it over the blood pounding in her ears. "I like that." He moved closer. "Very much."

He wasn't flirting, she was sure of that. He wasn't the type. No, Perses seemed more the type that cut straight to the chase and took what he wanted. Did he want her? She hitched a breath as the idea whirred around in her head, imagining those powerful arms holding her steady against the pillar, his mouth on hers, taking what he wanted.

"The bid stands at $45 million." Gemma blinked, her rampant sexual fantasy replaced by sudden shock. Omigod! Forty-five million! This was so far above the auction estimate it was beyond belief. She'd been so focused on Perses she hadn't heard the bids between.

She couldn't stop herself from bouncing on her heels like an excited teenager. "Omigosh! Did you hear *that*?"

He didn't answer, just adjusted his position so he could look down at her. Thoughtfully.

"Ladies and gentlemen, we have a phone bid of $50 million."

Gemma gasped as a hush fell across the auction room. This was the highest ever paid for a Bonvalet. "Do I hear $50 million and $100,000?" Silence.

"I'll take fifty." The room was pin-drop quiet. "Going once ... going twice ... this is your last opportunity, ladies and gentlemen." A long, agonizing wait as Mr. Rainey wearily scanned the room again and checked the row of McCallister's staff taking phone bids. All shook their heads. Finally, he banged his gavel. "Sold, for $50 million!"

Excited applause and chatter broke out across the room. "I wonder who bought it," Gemma asked, half to herself.

"You never told me."

"Sorry? Told you what?"

"Which boyfriend you mistook me for."

Drat, they were back to that again. Time to construct a lie that would put the matter to rest once and for all. "Actually, there's no point. He died."

"I see," he said. "And you thought he'd come back to life and you'd get reacquainted?"

Oh hell. Caught fair and square. "I have to go."

"Just a minute." This was a man used to being obeyed—and damned if her hot-to-trot body didn't like it. "Tell me what you really came here for."

As if he needed to ask. Going by his expression, he already had the answer.

"It was a mistake."

"It's never a mistake to get what you want."

"Except I ... I didn't come here for anything." What a blatant lie that was.

"Yeah, you did." His voice dropped to a sensual burr designed to tempt. "So perhaps we could ... ?"

The invitation permeated every pore in Gemma's overheated body, drawing her in, wrapping her in its sensual promise. Looking up, his eyes nailed hers. Intense. Commanding. He knew. He could take her right here, right now, and she probably wouldn't do a thing to stop him. Gemma forced her gaze away, trying desperately to expel the terrible, erotic thought.

This has to stop. Leave. Now!

But a heartbeat later, a powerful arm slid around her waist and she was bent back, giving him access to her mouth. It wasn't a long kiss, but the moment Gemma gasped against his lips and felt his tongue slip an inch inside her mouth to taste her, she knew Perses was taking what he wanted. His hold was so light it was almost at odds with his strength. An easy hold, but an all-claiming hold just the same. Enough to make a woman want to stay put. "Very nice," he murmured as he raised his head and his arm fell away. "My lookalike must have been one happy guy before he died."

Gemma was so shocked she couldn't speak. The man had tongue-kissed her. Just like that. As if he'd done nothing more than flick a stray hair off her shoulder.

He grinned. "So what killed him?"

Killed whom? Oh, dear Lord, now she had to think of some medical condition or something. "A paragliding accident," she mumbled, thinking fast. Surely that was tragedy enough to put an end to this whole conversation.

Another easy grin. Obviously, the man wasn't the "sorry for your loss" type.

"I see. How?"

Okay, he was playing with her like some damned toy; she got that. But she could play her own game. Closing her eyes, Gemma tried for grief stricken. "It was … " Her hand went to her forehead, overcome by the horrible memory, "in the Swiss Alps."

"Yeah? Did the harness break?"

Oh, he really intended to torture her. "I don't know … I guess it did." She dropped her hand and stared down at her pumps, working up her next fib, now furious with herself for starting this whole mess and, worse, at a loss on how to deal with him. "I wasn't there."

"Tough. How are you coping?"

Gemma kept her head down, wishing the floorboards would open up and take her straight to wherever her imaginary boyfriend had gone. "Fine," she shrugged, still staring at the floor.

"Did you have him flown back to the States?"

Dammit, enough of this. She met his gaze. "Actually, I have to …"

She lost her words when his dark, penetrating gaze stroked the length of her, pausing on her dress buttons. He was taking her again, letting her know she was his to play with. The man was dangerous all right, which in some strange, unsettling way only added to his sexiness. "I—I have to go back to the auction."

"I'm glad you got what you came for."

Sexy dangerous or not, he was a cocky devil. The overconfident type she didn't like. But even so, part of her did like him. Actually, most of her liked him—that was the trouble. Gemma put her nose in the air, determined to leave with whatever dignity she had left. "I don't know *what* you are talking about!"

He smiled at her lie, but then she knew he would. She also knew he was looking at her legs as she marched away, albeit slightly unsteadily. She knew it even before his low rumbling laugh swept away the last of her pride. "See you around, Sexy Legs."

Not if I see you first.

No way was she up for Perses again.

• • •

She was a masterpiece. A cascade of soft curls the color of midnight. Eyes as blue as the ocean. No, darker than the ocean. More like deep blue sapphires. And that skin. It was like a statue he'd once seen in a museum or somewhere. Yeah, alabaster, that was it, but soft with a hint of rose. Then there was her mouth—all soft and plump, just like a ripe, sun-kissed strawberry.

Jesus, talk about lame-assed thoughts. He knew fuck about art, but he knew what he liked—and this work of art had awakened his cock the minute he'd spotted her in that alcove. As it was, he was only at McCallister's on a job, but if auction houses housed delectable works like her, he'd come more often.

He watched her standing with a small group at the back of the room, sneaking looks across to him, her cheeks still pink from her adventure. Like some delicate, ebony-haired princess out of a fairy tale. He was too much of a bad boy to be a prince, but his kiss had aroused her, all right.

But who was she? Unless she came from family money, she was way too young to be a high-end art collector. Maybe twenty-five at the most. Besides, she was next to the kid who'd been given an earful by the auctioneer. Jamie? Yeah, that was it. It was more than likely she was a regular at McCallister's, so she wouldn't be difficult to track down.

She was still sneaking those looks, but now her arm was linked through the kid's. Her boyfriend? No, that was a friendship gesture more than anything. Or, maybe not. More like a show of defiance for his benefit. A visual "get lost" for kissing her. He might have felt bad about that if her lush mouth hadn't tasted so good.

She flexed a foot as she laughed at something Jamie said. Those legs were something, but then, so was the rest of her. Slender, with just the right amount of curviness to fulfill a man's fantasies. A pity she'd done up those buttons again.

An even bigger pity he hadn't asked for her number, even if it wouldn't have been forthcoming. But still, she might be up for dinner some night. Or, maybe with all that heat between them, they could just skip dinner and get right to it. It had been a while since he'd had the time to play.

He started toward her, carefully avoiding her line of sight. From the way she'd strode off, she'd probably bolt if she spotted him coming for her, and that would be a tragedy.

But hell if he wasn't losing his touch. He'd either miscalculated her sightline or she'd sensed him. Whatever it was, she quarter-turned her head in his direction, alarm rounding her blue eyes when she saw him closing in. For an instant, the blue met his before slipping downward, her attention snared for a split-second too long on his pants before she looked away. Yeah, that below-the-belt stare and red face said she was interested, all right. But it also said she was one embarrassed princess about to run.

Before he could reach her, she had pushed through the crowd and was out the nearest exit. Damn, she was fast.

Too late to catch her. He could always ask the kid who she was, but then again, there was probably no point. Sexual chemistry or not, the princess wasn't up for more playtime. Besides, she'd probably made the right decision, as much as he hated to admit it. She didn't come across as the casual pickup type, and he only did casual. But all the same, it was a pity.

CHAPTER TWO

One month later

"GG, old Stonebridge is on the warpath."

Gemma sighed and looked up from examining the signature on the small watercolor set up on her workbench. This was Lucy's third visit this morning. What was up with the girl?

"Lucy, shouldn't you be working?" She might as well be talking to the watercolor for all the good it did. Lucy's attention was now on Gemma's young colleague seated at the workbench.

"Hey, Jamie."

"Hey, Lucy."

Oh, right. Got it. Lucy had discovered Jamie O'Mara. Gemma had to hide her smile as she watched the two of them stare at each other like a pair of round-eyed opossums. Both were as pink as Lucy's tank top. Why was it that Gemma was always the last to figure these things out?

"Okay, Lucy, what about Maxim Stonebridge?"

Lucy leaned against the doorjamb and screwed up an eye in thought. To the uninformed, eighteen-year-old Lucy Barton might come across as a cent or two short of a dollar, but she was anything but, as most McCallister's employees found out within an hour of starting work. For a fact, almost nothing of interest slipped past Lucy's eyes or ears without being captured for the next water cooler tell-all. Although the teenager had been hired as an office assistant, Gemma had never actually seen her assisting anybody. The girl just floated about the place, sporadically working at her computer, making coffee, occasionally tidying the supply closet, or, like today, hanging around Gemma's workroom.

"Well, that's the thing, GG. I don't *know!*" she answered, chewing on a blond curl. This was a first. For once, the office snoop was stumped, and it was obviously annoying the hell out of her. "He stormed into John Allen's office five minutes ago, then stormed out again."

Gemma shook her head in resignation and went back to examining the signature. It looked genuine, but this was only the first of many tests.

"Jamie, are you going to find that signature list for me or not?" Not to put a damper on all that teenage yearning, but she did have an authentication to finish by the end of the week.

He jumped and bent his head to the signature book in front of him. "Sorry."

Gemma sighed, totally feeling like the third wheel. "Anyway, Lucy, it can't be very important if *you* don't know what's going on."

"That's true. Oh shit, here comes Cruella." Lucy's spine shot to attention as Maxim Stonebridge's executive assistant strode past her into the workroom, her face as red as a poppy. Something was up: Margot never came near the workrooms if she could possibly help it. She never went red either, for that matter.

"Gemma, Mr. Stonebridge wants to see you."

"Okay, I'll be there in five minutes. I just need to finish—"

Margot's voice soared to a decibel short of a shout. "*Now!*"

"What's going on?"

"Mr. Stonebridge will explain. Stop whatever you're doing, and come *right* now."

Just what she needed in the middle of her appraisal: a meeting with McCallister's chief executive, who, by all accounts, was fired up by something that couldn't wait five minutes. "Okay, I'm coming. Jamie, please check the signature list, and I'll follow up when I get back."

Slipping out of her white work coat—and wishing she hadn't worn casual Friday jeans midweek—Gemma followed Margot into the hallway. Lucy tugged at her sleeve.

"GG, *please* come and see me straight after your meeting."

"Haven't you got work to do, Lucy Barton?" Margot snapped, fixing the girl with a glare that could stop traffic. "Get back to whatever it is you do, although heaven *knows* what that is."

Gemma gave Lucy a wink and followed Margot into the elevator and up to the executive offices. Whatever was going on, it was enough to have the normally cool Margot on edge. The woman was tugging at her chain necklace like a lifeline. When the doors opened, Margot all but hurtled herself out of the elevator and into Maxim Stonebridge's office, tapping her foot impatiently while she waited for Gemma to catch up. By the time Gemma had come to a stop in the middle of the room, Margot was on her way out again, closing the door with an extra sharp click.

The room had the atmosphere of a funeral parlor. Maxim sat behind his oversized mahogany executive desk, his elderly, normally kind face ashen. John Allen, McCallister's operations manager, stood by the window, eyeing her coldly. The other man seemed familiar, but she couldn't place him. He looked as if he'd just bitten into a lemon.

Nobody invited her to sit, so she stood in the middle of Maxim's vast oak-lined office, twisting on her wedges, increasingly desperate for someone to say something.

It seemed to take forever before Maxim finally cleared his throat. "Philip, this is Dr. Gemma Gilmore, our lead authenticator for twentieth-century American paintings."

She started at the title. She was awarded her PhD in fine arts only three months ago, and it still came as a surprise when people called her "doctor." It was the first time Maxim had used it. At any other time, she might have felt proud of the unexpected acknowledgement. But at this moment, it felt forced. Out of place.

She stretched out a hand. "It's nice to meet—"

Her words were cut off as the man waved a hand in her direction, his expression incredulous. "This—this *girl*. You trusted *her?*"

"Dr. Gilmore has been with McCallister's since she came here as an intern. She's recognized internationally as an expert authenticator in her field. We have no reason to believe—"

"I don't care if she authenticated the goddamned Mona Lisa. She's *incompetent*."

Gemma started to feel weak. "What is this is about, Mr. Stonebridge?"

"The Frank Bonvalet Philip bought ... " McCallister's CEO, paused to draw a deep, shuddery breath before continuing. "It's a *fake*."

For a moment, Gemma thought her heart had stopped working. "Oh no, that's not poss—" The words died on her lips when Maxim rose slowly to his feet, bracing his hands on his desk for support. He stared at her numbly. "It's true. Philip received a tip-off that the painting is a forgery. This is a most unfortunate situation."

The blood drummed so hard in her ears, it felt as if her head had become a percussion instrument. "But ... " She stopped to run her tongue over her palate, seeking moisture in order to speak. "But I performed every possible authentication test on *Dreaming Atlantis*, along with weeks of research into the painting's history. There's no way it's a *forgery*." Oh God, the word sounded obscene.

Silence.

Why don't they say something?

Gemma watched dumbly as Philip Taurel began to pace the full length of Maxim Stonebridge's vast office, his fury permeating the room. Of course, she knew of Philip Taurel, but she had never actually met the billionaire and high-end collector of American art—one of McCallister's most valued buyers.

Taurel stopped his pacing and jabbed an accusing finger in Stonebridge's direction. "You let a kid authenticate a $50 million painting that I bought. You must be mad." Turning, he looked Gemma up and down, his eyes registering disgust as he took in her jeans. "Just *look* at her."

"Philip, we'll do everything we can," Stonebridge said.

"You'll do more than that. You'll refund my money today, or else I'll ruin you. By the time I'm finished, no collector in the world will touch your damned auction house."

John Allen stepped forward. "Mr. Taurel, we understand how you feel. We'll do a thorough investigation to find out how this could have happened. Once we know the full story, our insurers will, of course, pay you back every cent."

"I don't give a damn about your investigation or your insurers. You will write the check *now*!"

"You must understand," John continued patiently, "that our own experts must examine the painting first before we write a check for $50 million."

"Are you suggesting I'm lying?" Taurel turned back to Stonebridge. "You old fool. Did she spread her legs for you to get the job? I'll admit she's ... "

"That's enough, Taurel," came a deep rumble from somewhere behind Gemma's back. She blinked in shock, instantly recognizing the bourbon voice.

Horror filled her as Perses walked calmly across to Taurel, his big frame dominating the room, his expression hardened steel.

"Apologize."

She took an unsteady step forward to clutch the back of a chair. The room tilted and dipped. This couldn't be real. She was dreaming, and in a minute, she'd wake up. Except this was really happening. This was Perses fisting the lapel of Philip Taurel's jacket, his face inches away, shaking the man like he was made of rubber.

"I said apologize. *Now.*"

Taurel had turned almost as white as his business shirt. He said nothing, and Gemma thought he was going to pass out. But then he slumped a little, his voice ragged when he spoke. "I ... I apologize."

She stood in shock as Perses released Taurel's jacket and turned toward her. That he was here in Maxim Stonebridge's office wasn't the real horror. It was why he had stayed silent and hidden from her view that was upsetting. He wanted to see her reaction to the news about the Bonvalet, and from his expression, he didn't believe a word she'd said. Those scrutinizing eyes were now locked onto hers. Analyzing her. Judging her a liar. When they met a month ago, his eyes were sensual, teasing her when he'd taken what he wanted. Not a day had passed where she hadn't relived it, his arm imprisoning her, his mouth claiming hers. He'd scared her to the point of running away from him. Now he terrified her. She trembled as he took two long strides to reach her.

"I think Dr. Gilmore needs to sit down."

Sit down? No, she needed to escape this room. But his hand was under her elbow, propelling her to the chair. Somehow, Gemma found strength enough to yank her arm free from his grip, desperately trying to quell the rising dizziness. She could manage without him. She just needed to clear this whole thing up. Then go back to her workroom to finish her watercolor appraisal.

It ought to be easy.

"I don't need to sit down. Maxim, this can't be true. I worked for weeks on that painting, checking and rechecking. This is all a mistake."

Stonebridge rose to his feet, the disappointment in his eyes hurting her almost as much as the accusation. McCallister's had fast-tracked her career, placing complete trust in her ability. Everyone said she was good. More than good. *A genius*, they said.

That she possessed an extraordinary, almost uncanny ability to spot the smallest clue that a work was fake.

They'll be so embarrassed when they realize their mistake.

"There's no mistake, Dr. Gilmore," Stonebridge responded dully. "As of now, you are to cease all work at McCallister's. You're still on salary, but you will not come into the office until further notice, and you will not discuss this matter with anyone. Margot will be in touch. Now, if you will excuse us."

Gemma now knew for certain she was going to faint. But no way was she going to fall down in front of these men. They all assumed she was guilty of deliberately authenticating a forgery. In their eyes, she was a cheat and a liar. A criminal.

Wordlessly, she turned and started slowly for the door, concentrating on her every step. If she could just make it to the hallway, there was an empty office near the elevator. It had a sofa where she could lie down and take a few moments to think.

But she couldn't make it. She knew it even before she'd reached Margot's office and leaned helplessly against the wall, trying to breathe. Trying to control her despair.

She was swaying. Falling into blackness.

Strong arms lifted her.

Perses.

Through her misery and giddiness, she heard his deep, resonant voice above her head talking to someone. Probably Margot.

"I've got her."

Then she was being carried along the passage in those powerful arms—arms that curled tighter around her legs and waist as she tried to struggle. She dimly heard his order through her haze.

"Stay still."

It was useless. She couldn't fight him, and if he put her down on her feet, she had no confidence that she could stay upright anyway.

He laid her down on something soft. The sofa. She heard the door being closed, then felt a cushion slipped under her head, followed by the sound of a chair scraping on the hardwood floor. She could feel him just inches from her. Waiting in silence for her to respond. Opening her eyes, she tried to wrench herself upright, but a large hand on her chest pushed her back down.

"Don't even try. You're in shock."

"I'm fine," she tried to argue through trembling lips, her words falling away as lightheadedness swept her again.

"No, you're not. Believe me, I've seen it a hundred times."

"Seen people fainting?" she queried stupidly, latching on to something, anything, that would distract her from the horror of Maxim's office. "How? Where?"

She thought she saw his mouth ghost a smile, but then it was gone. It couldn't have been real because his brow was pulled so low. Fierce.

"Let's just say I've seen plenty of people go into shock. Sometimes, it's as simple as receiving news they didn't want to hear. Like you."

"Why are you here?"

That he didn't answer immediately was hope at least. It gave her precious time to think things through. Somehow, Philip Taurel had been given the wrong information about the Bonvalet. That's all it was. Misinformation. And despite the horror of it all, this could be cleared up. Perses didn't seem so scary now. His solid, almost calming presence reassured her. He'd helped her. Perhaps he believed her?

"Who are you're working for, Dr. Gilmore?"

Like she'd been tossed into an arctic sea to drown, all hope sank. "McCallister's, of course." So unconvincing when whispered through trembling lips, silly even, but maybe it was because she no longer had a place of work.

"Who else?"

She tried to sit up again, shrinking back when he shifted his weight toward her in warning. Perses was holding her prisoner.

"I don't know what you mean."

His hard stare didn't let up. It was futile to try and match such invincibility.

"No games. Who *else*?"

Oh yes, she *was* his prisoner, and he was interrogating her like an expert. Like this was his job.

Gemma's hackles rose in a desperate attempt at defense. "Are you going to beat it out of me?" So stupid, her show of defiance. She didn't feel defiant. Just suddenly tired and all used up and wanting to go back to her workbench to finish her appraisal. Except she couldn't go there. Not anymore.

"Beat you?" He looked so serious, she wondered for one horrible moment whether he might actually do it. "Maybe I should." His expression relaxed a fraction, but it didn't make him any less terrifying. "But you're still in shock, so I'll let it pass."

"Why won't you believe me? I don't know anything about a forgery."

"Princess, I don't buy a single word coming out your mouth. That act in Stonebridge's office was good, but not good enough."

Her breath froze in her throat. Surely he didn't actually believe those vile words?

"Why would I act? I didn't pretend to faint."

"Oh, you're in shock all right. Because you've been caught. Not in a million years would you have expected that. The forgery you authenticated was flawless. You really did your homework. Yeah, it was perfect. It was just bad luck for you there was a tip-off."

This was ridiculous. "Who are you talking about? The Bonvalet is genuine; I know it is."

He barely acknowledged her words. "It's likely the original has already been sold on the black market. No doubt the new owner will keep it hidden for a few years before putting it up for sale again. After years of dispute over ownership, nobody will be able to claim it. And of course, by then, it will be priceless."

A surge of anger put some fight back into her weakened mind. Attack was the best form of defense, right?

"You're a *liar*."

Gemma tried to swing her feet off the sofa to stand up, but he reached over, caught her ankle and held it fast. An iron grip utterly used to dealing with physical opposition; this was normal for him. The man could hold ten of her. Fear seeped through her defiance.

"Let me go."

"In time." He paused, and Gemma felt his thumb slide along her ankle. She tried to quell a shiver but failed. He must have felt it as he looked up, his thumb stilling as he watched her. Reading her. "The thing is, we thought it was the Wentworth that was fake. And I never expected it to be you."

"It's not me!"

He shrugged. "Of course, I figured there'd be someone at the auction. Seeing a forgery sold was just too good an opportunity to miss." He paused to look her over, slowly, methodically taking in every inch of her jeans and shirt. When he finally looked up, she caught the unmistakable flash of appreciation in his eyes. Her body warmed under the lingering appraisal. If he noticed, he didn't let it show. "But you? No, you had me fooled." His hand tightened its viselike grip as she moved to wrench her foot free. "Stay where you are."

"You're hurting me."

"Then don't move."

"Who *are* you?"

"Your worst nightmare until you tell me the truth." His words settled like ice on her skin.

"I *am* telling you the truth."

"The hell you are. But I'll get it out of you." He released her ankle. "Get up. I'll drive you home."

"I don't need your help," she retorted, gaining confidence at having her ankle back. Sitting up, Gemma rubbed at her leg, thankful she could finally escape her tormentor.

He laughed then. The same growling rumble she remembered from a month ago. Except now it was hard and cold, his ruthless eyes drilling hers.

"Believe me, princess, I'm not offering help here. Just the opposite. No way are you getting away to warn your colleagues."

She couldn't physically escape him, but she still had a mouth, right? "I don't have *colleagues*. Not the sort you mean, anyway. Let me leave right now, or I'll scream. I mean it."

"You can scream all the way to the parking lot if you want to." His voice dropped to a growl. "On your feet."

"No."

"You want me to carry you again?" He half-smiled, but it held no warmth.

She opened her mouth to retort but snapped it shut fast. He could toss her effortlessly into his arms. She might even like it, as much as she hated to admit the idea. Being trapped against him, his hand curled under her legs, the other crushing her to his chest. Every inch of him was sensual, raw power. That power was what had drawn her to him in the first place. Infuriatingly, it still drew her. Okay, so part of her wanted him. It didn't matter. She'd had the hots for good-looking men before. This was no different.

She fed him the strongest glare she could manage and got to her feet, trying to stabilize herself under the residual giddiness. "I can walk, thank you." How prim that sounded.

"That's a pity. Actually, I had intended to throw you over my shoulder."

And he'd do it without a second thought. It wouldn't matter to him if she was slung over his shoulder or dragged by her hair, kicking and screaming, all the way to the basement. Still, once she was home, she could slam the door in his face and then set about fixing this terrible misunderstanding with McCallister's. Perses hadn't said whom he worked for, but it couldn't be Philip Taurel. Not by the way Perses had threatened him. Forcing Taurel to apologize hadn't been chivalry. That wall of muscle standing before her didn't have a chivalrous bone in his body. No, his motivation had been something else.

She shrank back when he put out his hand. "Give me your phone."

He'd take it off her anyway, so she obeyed. Slipping it out of its holder attached to her jeans waistband, she held it at arm's length, almost dropping it through her trembling fingers. She watched him thumb through the display, checking recent calls, texts, contacts.

"You won't find anything," she muttered sullenly.

He handed it back. "If you try and use it, I'll take it off you for good." Opening the door, he waited while she tested her wobbly feet. "After you, Dr. Gilmore."

For a crazy split second, she had an overwhelming urge to make a run for it. If she could just make it to the elevator and close the doors, she'd lose him. But he was too close, shadowing her every step. He'd show no mercy. She'd be over his shoulder like a sack of corn, and somehow she didn't think screaming or pounding her fists into his back would save her.

"Excuse me, sir. I have Gemma's ... Dr. Gilmore's purse."

Was this some crazy conspiracy? Margot had actually gone to her workroom and collected her bag. They wanted her out of the building as of now. Like she was a criminal, not even trusted enough to collect her art books and photos and her favorite cashmere sweater she always left at work.

"Take it," was all he said, holding the purse out.

Her whole body shook when his big hand gripped her elbow again, steering her relentlessly toward the elevator.

"Margot, call the police," she pleaded over her shoulder, making a last, desperate attempt at escape. Surely that would stop him in his tracks.

Except her plea was ignored. Gemma heard Margot's heels rapping against the parquet floor all the way back to her office. Did nobody care that this terrifying man was kidnapping her? She felt sick with fear. He really meant this.

"Who are you?"

He smiled grimly. "We'll get acquainted soon enough."

CHAPTER THREE

His plan hadn't worked.

He'd scared her all right, but not into confessing. Gemma Gilmore might not fit his usual suspect profile, but no way was she going to make this easy.

Being rough with her might have been necessary, but he didn't feel good about it. This woman—now standing in her kitchen, where she'd fled to escape him—was made for other things. Things that he'd ached to do since he'd first spotted her in that alcove at McCallister's. Like explore those soft, delicate curves. Taste that full mouth again. Look into those incredible, blue eyes when she welcomed him into her body.

Except that wasn't going to happen anytime soon, despite the heat between them. The princess was looking at him like he was the devil himself, eyes wide and wary, primed and ready to bolt for the door if he gave her half a chance.

He knew from experience that if she were going to confess, it would need to be in the next few minutes while she was still too numb with shock to think straight. He was lucky to have her scared at all. After Taurel had insulted her and he'd stepped in, she might have lost her fear. It had been a risk, but he couldn't let Taurel—or anyone else for that matter—speak to her like that. Even now, he had to fight the urge to show her a kinder side. To help her instead of interrogating her until he got the truth. He stood in the middle of her tiny apartment and watched her struggle to open a bottle of Perrier, her hands trembling so hard that, in the end, she gave up. Yeah, Dr. Gilmore was all shocked to hell, but that was understandable. If her impressive international reputation was anything to go by, her work was her whole life— and her life had just blown apart.

In his work, he'd never come close to meeting a woman like her. They were worlds apart, but even so, he could see the similarities. Gemma Gilmore had talent and ambition—the very things that his superiors had identified and cultivated in him. He smiled ruefully to himself. Under other circumstances they might have liked each other.

"Let me," he offered, shrugging off his jacket and taking the few steps to the kitchen. She backed away to maintain distance from him.

He gestured to a shelf behind her. "Glass?"

She didn't argue. Just turned and took a tumbler down, setting it on the countertop, her gaze focused on every movement of his hands as he undid the bottle and filled the glass. He might have felt a little sorry for her, but he couldn't afford to offer sympathy.

He held out the water for her. She took it, her hand now shaking so hard she had to set the glass down on the countertop.

"Take it easy, Dr. Gilmore. I don't bite." He quirked a small smile to ease her anxiety just enough so she could speak. "Except when it's a medium-rare steak."

Surprisingly, she almost smiled back. The tiniest upward flicker, nothing more, but dammit if it didn't put him on the back foot— and not for the first time with this woman.

"That's better. Just relax."

She stayed silent, so he went on, trying to focus his thoughts. He couldn't believe how much she affected him. Invaded his senses.

"You can get through this, Gemma." He paused, waiting while she registered the use of her name. "I know it seems like the end of the world right now, but people get sucked into things they normally wouldn't do." He slid his fingers under her chin to ease her head back, waiting until she met his gaze before continuing. "Is that how it was?"

She blinked at the question. "No ... I—this is crazy."

"We know all about it. The planning. The people involved. We just need a few gaps filled." He dropped his voice. Made it soft. "Can you do that for me? Fill those gaps?"

"Are you police?"

Damn, she was starting to think through the situation. It wouldn't take her long to realize they had no real proof of her involvement. And she'd be right. The forgery was so good she could simply say she'd got it wrong. Yeah, it was a meticulously planned and executed job. Chasing down art forgers wasn't his usual line of work, but he'd been put on forced leave after his last grueling mission and was happy to take on an easy job. But this was not as easy as he'd expected. The Wentworth was genuine and, assuming the tip-off to be false, they'd closed the case. Until yesterday. Now it was complicated and about to get even more complicated. Dr. Gilmore was no longer in shock. Now she was all wide-eyed suspicion.

Ready for him.

"Why were you in Venice three months ago?"

Her eyes flashed surprise, then anger. "Have you been *following* me?"

In truth, McCallister's personnel manager had provided the information minutes before the meeting in Stonebridge's office, though he couldn't afford to tell her that detail. He needed her to think she'd been tailed for months. "Not me personally, although I might have enjoyed that. *Answer* me."

"I was there on vacation," she snapped defiantly.

There had to be more. He took a punt.

"We know who the guy is." He fixed his eyes on her breasts to distract her. Under that white linen shirt, the hint of a pink bra was distracting the hell out of him.

She blushed. At least he had her unsettled again, although she was looking at him like he was some predator. Hell, he felt like some goddamned predator. He wanted to taste every inch of her.

"How do you know him?"

"He's ... he's just a friend."

Yeah, he was right. She'd gone to Venice with a man.

"Was he a good fuck?"

"You *pig*!" The word shot out of her mouth so fast he knew her reaction was genuine. "He's better than you'd ever be, that's for sure."

Whoa, that went better than expected. All fired up, and with a little luck, she'd blow a fuse any second and blurt something out.

"Hey, a friend with benefits is a good thing. Gets rid of all that pent-up frustration. Who else have you been doing? An art forger?"

"*Get out!*"

He didn't move. Just waited while she worked out what to do next. If he didn't know better, she could pass for innocent. But being the best in her field, there's no way could she have mistaken the forgery for the real thing.

"How much did he pay you to authenticate the fake?"

"Go to hell!" She started to push past him toward the door, then stopped, her body inches from his, staring straight ahead at his chest. He held his breath, waiting, knowing what was about to happen. She was angry and confused, but she was also turned on by his roughness. He'd seen it a hundred times. That fine line between loathing and lust. Yeah, she was stuck in limbo all right, deciding whether to do something about her arousal or order him out.

"You want me to kiss you again, sweetheart?"

His endearment caught her completely off-guard. Her gaze fell in embarrassment, then, perhaps realizing it might look like a crotch stare, flew quickly back to his chest. A pity she hadn't looked. If she had, she'd have seen exactly what was on his mind.

"Perses." The word exhaled from her mouth on a wisp of breath—so soft, he barely caught the sound. A code name?

He tilted her head back again, trying to read her expression. "Tell me what that means." With a small shiver, she angled her face into his hand, closing her eyes in surrender. The air between them was electric. Heavy. "Tell me, Gemma," he repeated softly.

Then she smiled, as if holding some delicious secret. A gentle curve of her beautiful mouth that took his breath away and had him slipping his arm around her small waist, splaying his fingers flat across her back to draw her softness to him. Her body quivered under his hand. This wasn't fear. It was desire. "What's making you smile?"

"Your name."

"What? Perses?"

She gave a barely perceptible nod. "The Titan god of destruction."

He couldn't help but smile at that. True, he'd destroyed a few things in his time, so, yeah, it kind of fit. With his free hand, he tangled his fingers in her long mane of raven hair, forcing her head back to look into her eyes. She fought to avoid his gaze, but he held her firmly, until finally, the azure pools lifted to his and he knew there was no turning back. Neither of them would be able to stop this until sated. His interrogation had failed. He needed some other way to get her to open up.

This way.

He kissed her, his blood turning to fire as she responded. Tasting him. Welcoming his tongue into her mouth. Her hands fisted his shirt as she pushed high on her toes to press her belly against his erection.

"Bedroom?" he barked.

Her eyes slid toward the half-open door to his right.

"Beside you."

He half-turned. Shit. Wasn't that a closet or something? No way could they fit in there. Well, if he had to bang her standing up, so be it.

Slipping his hands under her arms, he lifted her straight up to his height, grunting in approval when her legs went around his waist, her mouth finding his as he carried her through to her tiny bedroom. He heard her shoes clatter to the floor behind him.

The bed was barely big enough for him, let alone the two of them, but he could work around that. Plunking her down on her back, he started on her jeans. Yeah, it was fast, unromantic, but he needed her now. He'd explore every inch of her later.

But getting her stripped was like getting past some God-awful chastity belt. Fucking skinny jeans. Wrenching the zipper down, he grabbed two fistfuls of denim and worked the material over her hips, cursing at every yank. At least she raised her hips to help, although he had the impression she was laughing at him. Then the sight of a scrap of pink underwear distracted him. The thing couldn't cover a flea's ass. As he curled his fingers around the flimsy lace, it stretched, snapping in his hand.

"Jesus, you're beautiful," was all he could say at the sight of her. The battle with her jeans was worth the effort. Even half-stripped, she was exactly how he'd imagined her. Pale and slender, with surprisingly long legs for a woman of barely medium height. A waxed pussy, except for a landing strip. Exactly how he liked them. Hell, he liked every inch of her.

He sat down on the edge on the bed. It squeaked in protest at his weight. This was all he needed. A noisy ride. If her neighbors were home, they were in for a treat.

Leaning over her, he kissed her, slipping his hand between her legs to explore. Dear God, just a touch of her wetness could make him come. He'd happily go down and take a taste of her right now, but every cell in his body screamed for release. Standing, he grabbed a condom from his wallet before shedding his clothes, shoes, and socks, aware of how her eyes took him in. He liked that hungry stare way more than he should.

By the time he'd rolled the condom on, she'd kicked off her jeans and was waiting for him, legs drawn up, knees wide apart. Christ, she was a sexy thing.

He didn't waste time with his shirt. Or hers. Settling himself between her legs, he ignored the bed's loud screech and propped himself up on his elbows. He'd thought about her for weeks but held off finding out who she was. Now, he could barely believe she was in his arms.

Sliding his hand down between them, he kept his eyes locked on hers as he notched his cock against her entrance, feeling her wetness opening to him. He closed his eyes, savoring the feel of her before working further into her, loving the sensation of her body closing around him. He withdrew a little, preparing for the slide all the way home, when he felt her tense. Hell, was he was hurting her?

"Are you okay?"

"You're big," she whispered.

He rasped a laugh. "Yeah, that's me." Even holding himself completely still and only half inside her, she felt impossibly good. Like no woman he'd ever had—and there'd been more than he cared to remember.

Gently, he eased further in, now thankful for the slow pace. He needed slow. But then she suddenly wrapped her legs around his hips and pushed herself up in invitation, so he drove all the way in. She tensed a little, and he held still, waiting until he could feel her relaxing under him. Finally, at his limit, he slipped a hand under her ass and, lifting her hips, thrust hard—maybe too hard, too deep, but her core opened more with every stroke, so he kept going.

Her head hit the headboard. She trembled, huffing against his neck.

He froze. "Sorry, I'm a rough bastard. Are you ... ?"

A firm dig of her heels in his butt was answer enough.

He exhaled with relief. Delicately made, but she could take him.

With a low growl, he gripped her plump little ass again to hold her steady as he bucked into her. The bed sagged and groaned in protest.

He stilled again, hating the loss of momentum. Hell, if the damn thing collapsed, he really would have to take her standing up. Either that, or on the floor.

Pushing himself up to rest his palms on each side of her shoulders, he grinned down at her. "Will you mind if I break your bed?"

Her hands slid up around his neck, drawing him down, matching his grin with one of her own. "If you do, you'll have to buy me a new one."

He chuckled, trying to remember when he'd last laughed out loud during sex. It felt good. "Deal." Angling his head to reach her mouth for a slow kiss, he surged into her heat again, her hips undulating up to him, her heels on his butt urging him deeper into her body. A few hard strokes later and she threw her head back with eyes closed, clawing at his shirt, meeting him stroke for stroke. She was close, and dammit, he was going to look into those eyes when she came.

"Oh God," she moaned, and he knew she was at the point of no return.

"Look at me." He didn't think she'd heard him, but at the exact moment she crested, her eyes flickered open, letting him revel in the dark sapphires locked on his gaze as he felt every muscle in her core squeezing him in waves of exquisite pressure. He tried to hold back, delay the sweet release, but she was too much. Too incredible. A split second later, he exploded into her.

For minutes they lay still, their erratic breathing the only sound between them. He broke the silence first.

"You need a bigger bed."

"It belongs to my grandmother. A family heirloom." She sighed against his neck.

"Oh."

"Your tattoo. What is it?"

"Celtic dragon."

"It's nice," she murmured.

He kissed her hair, surprised at how much he liked her interest and the feel of her face snuggled against his throat. He could happily stay like this, but even on his elbows, she had to be feeling his weight. So he rolled out, disposed of the condom, and then made himself as comfortable as he could in her grandmother's ridiculously undersized bed.

"Sorry about your underwear."

She didn't answer—just nestled her face into his shirt, her fingers drawing a pattern around each button before undoing it to explore his chest. That he was enjoying her so much worried the hell out of him. Years of intelligence work had taught him to be cautious. Never trust. Never get involved. He'd broken every rule in the manual with her. This wasn't even a one-night-stand situation. Those he could deal with. His choice of job made it impossible for him to have a woman in his life. But for the first time, a woman had caught his interest to the point where he wanted more than just the sex, as good as it was. He wanted to know her. What made her tick. Why would she get involved in an art fraud when, at twenty-five, she was near the top of her career ladder and still climbing? It didn't make sense.

He sucked in a sharp breath as her small fingers fluttered down over his belly, then slid along his still half-erect cock, gently teasing it back to hard. He closed his eyes and sank into the pleasure of her soft hand.

"You're beautiful," she whispered, tracing a fingertip around the ridge before slipping her hand down the shaft again. "You like that?"

Oh yeah, he liked it.

"Uh-huh," he managed to answer, closing his eyes again as she built a steady rhythm. Whatever her past, she sure knew how to pleasure a man. With this excuse for a bed, he'd assumed she hadn't seen much action in it.

But silky-warm hand or not, he needed to finish what he'd started. Sliding his hand up under her shirt, he worked his fingers under her bra to cup a breast. His fingers told him she had the kind of breasts he liked. Not big, but curvy. Just right for a slender thing like her. Tweaking at the tight bud of a nipple, he felt her bow up to him, her hand slipping off his cock. At least he could concentrate now.

"Take off your shirt." No way did he trust himself to do it. He'd already ruined her panties, or thong, or whatever the hell it was.

Sitting up, she obediently unbuttoned her shirt, tugged it off, and tossed it over the end of the bed, all the while watching him from under a screen of dark lashes. It was hard to tell what she was thinking, but she was ready for more of him—that much was obvious. He dragged his own shirt off, sending it in the same direction.

"And the bra." Pink. Lacy. Hell, ordering a woman out of her bra had never been so sexy. She undid the hook between the cups, now staring hard at his abs and everything below, while he enjoyed his own view. But mutual admiration would have to wait. With a grunt of satisfaction, he laid her down, sparks going off in his brain when she stroked his cock again. Man, she was made for him. And right now he was going to taste her. Every inch of her.

"Do you work for Philip Taurel?"

His mouth had only just found a nipple when her question stopped him in his tracks.

"No."

She squirmed as his tongue went back to work on the rosy peak. "McCallister's?"

"It doesn't matter who I work for." Definitely not when his cock was iron and his balls ached for release again. He kissed his way across to the other nipple, gently drawing the nub between his teeth, enjoying her small moan of pleasure as she rose up for more. That should keep her preoccupied until he was ready to give her more answers.

"Why don't you believe me about the Bonvalet?"

Shit. He looked up. Her face was flushed with her arousal, but her eyes were keenly focused on his reaction, rather than where he'd prefer them to be. He didn't need this. Not with her spread out for him like this, testing him to the limit.

"Do you want to talk about paintings, or do you want to do this?" Hell, he knew what he wanted. He wanted to investigate that landing strip and everything below. With his mouth.

Her eyes went round and innocent-looking. "Why can't we do both? Who do you work for?"

"Hey, I think maybe we'd better call this quits." As much as he hated to admit it, she was getting way too clever with her questions.

She pushed up on her elbows, a small, coquettish smile playing at the corners of her mouth. "I'm sorry. Please don't stop."

"Right. Well, where were we?"

Slipping down the mattress, his legs went over the end of the bed, jamming his feet against the wall. Pushing her legs up over his shoulders, he kissed his way along the inside of each soft thigh before drawing his tongue slowly along her sex, keeping it gentle, knowing she'd still be sensitive from her orgasm. Sensitive and begging for more, by the way she was trembling under his mouth. So wet and beautiful. Man, he was going to enjoy this. Keep her coming until he couldn't stand it for another moment and he'd have to climb back up her beautiful body and fuck them both to oblivion.

His mouth had barely gotten busy when the next question came.

"Who do you work for?"

Okay, that was it. She might be made for him, and he might be hornier than he'd ever been in his entire life, but enough was enough. He was being played.

Pulling himself up, he wedged himself between her and the wall, slipping an arm under her to make more room for himself.

"Who do *you* work for, princess?" He tried to keep his voice even, but a mix of irritation and lust had made him hoarse.

He felt her sigh against his shoulder. "I answered your questions, Perses. Now answer mine."

When she tried to reach down and stroke his cock, he grabbed her hand and held it firmly. No way did his dick need more stimulation.

"But you didn't answer my questions, Dr. Gilmore. When you do, maybe we can get back to other matters."

"But I can take you or leave you, Perses." He felt her lashes fluttering against his chest. "So I don't need your ... *other matters.*"

He laughed at that and released her hand to lightly caress a breast. She had plenty of spirit for sure. He liked it.

"Yeah, you do. You're just dying for me to get back down there and give you the best orgasm you've ever had." Jesus, he meant it. He'd give her twenty orgasms. Right now. Once she'd told him what he wanted to know.

"You mean better than the last?" She slid down his chest, kissing her way over his pecs, her fingers slowly tracing around each abdominal. "If you insist. But first, tell me what you know about the Bonvalet fraud."

Reality hit him like an out-of-control freight train. This wasn't some game where they could play-fuck information out of each other. In some strange way, she'd done him a favor with her questions.

Climbing over her, he got to his feet and started dressing, aware that she hadn't moved, except to pull a corner of the sheet over herself. She was clearly confused about what had just happened, but that wasn't so bad. In the next three minutes, she'd think him a complete bastard—and she'd be right.

He was dressed when he sat down on the edge of the bed to talk to her. "I want you to listen to me carefully. We know there's an American link to the fraud. It's you." He saw her mouth open to protest, but he kept going before she could speak. He needed her scared and vulnerable again. "Our informant told us about the connection to McCallister's." He paused, letting the words sink in, seeing the fear creep back into her eyes.

"You didn't mistake that forgery for the real thing. You're up to your neck in this, and I'm going to get the truth. If you think a roll in the hay changes anything, it doesn't. It was nice, but that's all it was. No, the best thing you could do is give me the name of the forger you met in Venice, before the police, FBI, and whoever else comes after you. And they *will* come after you."

She didn't confess. She didn't even shout a denial. She just looked stunned, like she had in Stonebridge's office. Sliding herself down in the bed, she turned to face the wall, curling her legs up against her body.

Her voice was small when she finally spoke. "Go away."

He took a card from his wallet. "Here's my number, Gemma, when you're ready to talk. Make it soon. My name's Mack Buchanan, by the way."

At the door, he turned to look at her. She hadn't moved, except to scrunch the sheet up to her face. Maybe she was crying.

Not the first time he'd felt bad about doing his job. But this time it hurt.

Hurt like hell.

CHAPTER FOUR

She'd had sex with her enemy, and his name was Mack Buchanan.

Gemma still couldn't get her head around the fact that she'd done it. By giving into her desire for him, all she'd gotten was an orgasm. Nice, but not very useful when it came to finding out what was going on. She should have realized the man wasn't the pillow-talk type. Of course he wouldn't have fallen for her obvious "please tell me everything, Perses" routine. She'd made a mistake. But then, she'd never experienced such an incredible sexual chemistry with anyone—and if she were being totally honest with herself, she'd do it again in an instant. There had to be something wrong with her.

"Sorry I'm late."

Gemma jumped, nearly spilling her coffee across the café table. It was Lucy—grinning from ear to ear, her dark blonde hair dragged into a rough ponytail, sunglasses perched on the top of her head. There was something comforting about the sight of Lucy. As if the world hadn't turned upside down after all.

"So did he arrest you, GG?"

But there was no doubt about it: The girl never felt a sliver of sympathy for the plight of others.

"That Mack Buchanan is huge," Lucy breezed on, flopping down in the chair opposite and signaling for the waitress. "God, when he dragged you into the elevator, I thought you were a goner for sure. But what a way to go. *So* seriously drop-dead gorgeous."

"How on earth do you know about that? Were you watching?" A dumb question. The girl could run a five-star detective agency with her surveillance skills.

From Lucy's exasperated expression, Gemma's IQ had just dropped fifty points. "Of course! Cappuccino, please," she instructed the waitress before leaning over the table, her brown eyes round with interest. "So, where'd he take you, GG?"

"Home." That was all Lucy was going to get by way of information. As it was, that was probably too much.

"Is that all? Well, anyway, let me fill you in."

Gemma sat back and waited. No doubt Lucy knew something useful. In fact, that was the reason Gemma had texted her to meet after work in the café, two blocks from McCallister's. Her banishment from the office meant she needed a source of information. And what better source than an inquisitive, gabby teenager? The only problem would be keeping Lucy quiet about their meeting. Lucy's mouth didn't do discreet.

"Okay, so what's going on at the office?"

"Well ... the thing is—jeez, you look awful. There are, like, huge *shadows* under your eyes."

Lucy didn't do tactful either.

"Rough night, sweetie. Go on."

Rough night indeed. After Mack had left, Gemma barely made it to her bathroom before throwing up from guilt and shame and every other raw emotion left in her. Crawling back to bed, she'd spent hours reliving the nightmare of the whole day, until finally she took an Ambien that knocked her out for what seemed like ten minutes but was instead a few hours. Then, at four in the morning, it had started again. The swarming memories, the terror that seemed to come out of the very walls of her bedroom, sabotaging her every attempt to understand how she could have authenticated a forgery.

But the humiliating memory of letting him play with her had been almost as bad. Oh yes, he'd had his fun with her, his roughness morphing into one big, erotic turn-on. The kisses, the touches, the weight of his powerful body, his—

"Of course he was back in the office this morning."

Gemma blinked. "Who?"

Lucy shook her head impatiently. "Pay attention. Sex-on-a-stick Buchanan, of course. Went straight to John Allen's office and closed the door. I think old Stonebridge is sick or something. He wasn't in today, and Cruella is so grouchy. You know, she actually ordered me off the executive floor. Can you *believe* it?"

Gemma briefly closed her eyes, trying to filter out Lucy's ramble from the important fact that Mack had been at McCallister's talking to John Allen. Presumably, that meant John knew something, whatever that was.

Lucy's voice prattled on. "It's not like I report to her or anything. She *knows* that."

"Sweetie, no one knows who you report to."

Lucy's chin shot straight out with indignation. "That's not fair!"

"Listen, Lucy, I want you to do something for me. But ..." She paused; this could be a mistake. The trouble was there was no one else to trust with the job, or, for that matter, anyone else prepared to do it. Well, she would just have to risk asking. "I need the Bonvalet notes from my workroom. They're in the filing cabinet under the window. Do you know the one?"

Lucy rolled her eyes. "I *know* where the notes are."

"You do? How? No matter. Anyway, can you get them without anyone knowing?"

"Of course!"

"Great. Text me when you have them, and we'll arrange to meet. The thing is I'm asking you to do something risky, so I'd understand if you—"

"No problem. So, how did that old billionaire Taurel find out about the forgery?"

Lord, was there no end to this girl's information-gathering skills? "You know about that? I never said—"

"Sometimes you're so slow, GG. I overheard John Allen talking to Margot in her office. She always leaves the door open. That's when she told me to get lost," she explained, then snorted in disgust.

"You absolute darling. So what else did you hear?"

The waitress set Lucy's cappuccino on the table, so Gemma had to wait patiently while Lucy stirred her coffee, sipped, emptied two packets of sugar into the cup, and stirred again. How the girl managed to stay bean-thin was anyone's guess.

"Actually, not much. John was going on about Big Mack investigating, that's all."

"Did John say who Big Mack—I mean Mack Buchanan— works for?"

Lucy chewed on a nail while she thought. "Um, no ... nothing like that. But Cruella kicked me out right about then, so I missed the rest."

"You have to keep this quiet, Lucy. You understand that, don't you?"

"Oh sure, but Jamie knows."

"*How*?"

"I told him, silly. Actually there is something I want to ask you, GG." Lucy worked a loose curl into the corner of her mouth and gnawed, always a sign that something was wrong in her world. "The thing is ... "

Oh, hell. She'd blabbed. Who else would she have told about the painting? Another dumb question. Everyone.

"Go on," Gemma prompted, bracing herself for the bad news.

"Well, here's the thing ..." Lucy paused, so Gemma reached over and gave her fingers an encouraging squeeze—although what she really wanted to do was shake the girl's brains out.

"It's okay. Just *tell* me."

Lucy smiled weakly and released the curl from her mouth. "Do you think I should ask Jamie on a date?" she blurted out, her face turning bright pink. "He's gorgeous, but he won't ask me. I know he likes me."

For the first time since her nightmare began, Gemma found herself laughing. Poor Lucy. All gone to pieces over a boy. A very cute boy at that. "Oh, Lucy, of course you should. He's just shy."

Lucy's brown eyes flashed relief. "Really? He hasn't got a girlfriend, and he's not gay. I checked."

"How did you ... ?" She stopped, deciding she really didn't need to know. "You are amazing." She laughed again when Lucy frowned as if hearing the obvious. "Anyway, ask him out. Of course he'll say yes."

"Okay, I will! Actually, I have to go. I promised to make tacos tonight." Her voice dropped to a conspiratorial whisper. "I'll text you as soon as I have the notes. My first real assignment. This is, like, *sooo* cool."

Despite the seriousness of the situation, Gemma couldn't help but see the humor in having Agent Lucy on the job. Never mind that Gemma's reputation was all shot to hell and her career practically over. As far as Lucy was concerned, this was one big, exciting drama.

"A regular Veronica Mars, that's you. But *please,* keep this quiet. I mean it, Lucy. Promise me."

"Yeah, yeah, I get it."

The trouble was Lucy didn't get it. Gemma sighed as she watched her enthusiastic recruit weave her way between the tables to the exit, her ponytail bouncing higher than usual in her excitement. Of course Lucy would get her notes, and, with a bit of luck, she might be able to keep quiet about it, at least until the investigation was over. If McCallister's found out, both of them would be fired without a moment's notice and the police called. But Lord knows she had to do this. Her technical analysis notes held every detail about the Bonvalet. There might be something she'd missed in her carefully documented annotations. Something to put to rest the nagging, worrying thought that, despite her reassurances to Maxim Stonebridge that the painting was genuine, it could be a fake after all. One thing was for sure. There *was* a forgery out there, and it was either with Philip Taurel or somewhere in Italy. If nothing else, knowing which was which would give her closure.

Closure that could see the end of her career.

• • •

"What the hell is going on?"

Gemma stepped back from the door, too dazed by the question to even attempt an answer. She watched dumbly as her ex-fiancé strode into her apartment, his face thunder. Whatever he had to say, it wasn't anything she wanted to hear.

"Well?" he continued, glaring around her apartment as if the very walls hid some national secret.

She couldn't stop her irritation. They hadn't spoken for weeks, but here he was, bursting in without so much as a hello.

She put a hand on her hip. "Well, what?"

"Some guy came to my office late this afternoon. Big, solid guy—around six foot three. Early thirties. Said he was investigating a matter at McCallister's. You'd better start explaining what the hell you're mixed up in."

Mack Buchanan. Could her worst nightmare get any worse? He had actually gone to Kyle's office, probably around the same time she'd met Lucy at the café. The man really intended to follow through on his threats. But digging into her personal life to the extent of questioning Kyle at his work? That she didn't need on top of everything else.

Damn him.

Kyle thundered on, not waiting for an explanation. "Just walked straight into my office while I was with a client, acting like a cop or something! What's going on?"

She felt a pang of guilt. Kyle didn't deserve this, even though he was glaring at her like she'd just hit number one on *America's*

Most Wanted. Truthfully, she couldn't blame him for being pissed. A top-ranked lawyer with the most prestigious law firm in New York didn't need that jerk paying him a visit.

"So, what did he say?"

"Told the client to excuse us, said his name was Buchanan, then started throwing a lot of questions at me about Venice. Why I'd been there with you. How long I'd known you. It was liked some cross-examination. I told him to get out or I'd call security, but he couldn't have cared less. I'll tell you this much: the guy looks like he can handle himself."

Nothing like a brutal reminder. He'd handled her all over.

Gemma sank down on the sofa, trying to think through the situation.

"So what did you tell him?"

Kyle dragged his fingers through his fair hair. "I told him we'd been on vacation." He walked across to the sofa and sat beside her. "Venice? Why the hell would he want to know about that?"

Because he thinks I met an art forger there.

Venice. A relationship-repair vacation, that's what the trip had been about. In one of the most romantic cities in the world—except not even Venice couldn't fix her falling out of love. Strange to think that she would be married to Kyle by now if things had gone according to plan. She'd be living in his plush Manhattan apartment instead of her tiny studio.

A fine man from a good family, just thrown away, her snobbishness-prone mother still reminded her whenever she got the chance. As far as her mother was concerned, if Gemma had paid more attention to Kyle instead of working 24/7 to finish her PhD in record time, he wouldn't have gone off in desperation and had an affair.

Desperation? As far as she could see, there hadn't been anything desperate about Kyle's cheating. She'd met Kyle at a gallery opening two years ago. She had been there with her mother, who recognized Kyle from the news. He'd been the lead defense counsel in a high-profile trial involving a congressman accused of murdering his wife. The case had been the talk of New York for months. Kyle had won the case and become famous. As far as her mother was concerned, money and fame made him perfect husband material. Within minutes, they'd been introduced.

You can't do better than a lawyer, her mother had enthused all the way home, *especially one who's going places—to the top, from what I hear*. Until Kyle, her mother had always dismissed Gemma's boyfriends as too unambitious. And the next day, Kyle called Gemma to invite her to dinner.

Yes, she *had* loved him. And he was ideal husband material—no one could deny that. Stylish. Wealthy. And *nice*.

She stared down at Kyle's long, slim fingers holding hers. He had nice hands. A nice body from his regular gym workouts. Everything about Kyle was nice: from his fair hair and blue eyes to his immaculate business suits. Maybe that had been the trouble. He was *too* nice.

She briefly closed her eyes, trying but failing to prevent the inevitable comparison with the man who'd been in her bed yesterday. That brute was more rough edges than nice. What her mother would think of him, Gemma couldn't begin to say. But it wouldn't be much, in all likelihood.

"Did he ask about anything else? A forgery, for instance?"

"No, nothing like that," Kyle answered, his head dropping a little while he thought. He looked up. "*What* forgery?"

Telling Kyle everything would be another risk. A whiff of scandal would scare the hell out of Cooper & Forney's top criminal lawyer, especially now that he'd just made senior partner. Any suggestion that he was involved in an art fraud would be enough to send him into a panic. But Kyle wouldn't leave without an explanation, so she might as well tell him everything. Except for one detail. That wasn't for sharing.

"McCallister's sold a Frank Bonvalet landscape a month ago. *Dreaming Atlantis*. I authenticated it. Except, it's ... " Gemma scrunched a breath, still unable to say the word without her stomach curdling, "a fake."

"Oh, good Lord. How the hell did that happen?"

Kyle asking the obvious didn't help her anxiety.

"That's just it—I don't know. Maybe I did get it wrong. The thing is McCallister's thinks I deliberately verified the fake as genuine and that I was in Venice to meet with the forger."

She closed her eyes against Kyle's huff of irritation. "You'd better tell me everything. From the beginning."

Gemma paused to organize her explanation; every word needed to be clear and straightforward for Kyle's legal mind. He always got impatient when she dithered.

Taking a deep breath for steadiness, she started. "The Bonvalet went to that billionaire businessman—you know the one—Philip Taurel. Anyway, yesterday I was called to Maxim's office, and Philip Taurel was there with John Allen. Maxim told me Taurel's painting is a forgery. Of course, I told him it wasn't possible. That I did every test to ensure its authenticity." She stopped, realizing she was gabbling.

Kyle nodded. "Go on."

"Well, anyway, the guy who came to see you, Mack Buchanan, was there as well. I don't know who he is or who he works for. He said it wasn't McCallister's, but it must be. Well, he ... " She stopped again to work through her next words. No way must anyone know about her indiscretion, especially her ultraconservative ex. It wouldn't matter that they'd broken up months ago; he'd still be disgusted at her leaping into bed with a total stranger. She didn't feel up to defending her actions.

"He asked me about why I'd been in Venice, that's all," she finished.

Kyle's eyebrows went up. "In that case, why does he think I'm involved?"

"I suppose because we were there together, he thinks you're mixed up in it, somehow."

"Have you gone to the police?"

Gemma shook her head, although she was starting to wonder if she should. Maybe they'd help her with a protection order against Mack Buchanan. Although that wasn't likely, given she didn't know who he was, where he lived, or who he worked for.

"I guess McCallister's will bring the police into this, eventually," she said, gnawing at her lip. "They must be terrified of this coming out. It would mean every painting I've authenticated would have to be checked."

"Can't you meet with Stonebridge to explain?"

"I'm banned from the office until further notice." She frowned. "Does Miranda know you're here?" Miranda being the stunning colleague who had consoled him while Gemma was working so hard on her PhD. Of course, it wasn't necessary to bring Miranda into the conversation. Kyle hardly mentioned her, but even so, her name still hung between them whenever they talked.

Oh, he'd had plenty of excuses for having an affair with the firm's newest, prettiest intern. Miranda meant nothing to him, he'd insisted, as if that somehow made it okay. He'd even tried to guilt-trip her: Miranda wouldn't have happened if Gemma had spent more time with him. If she'd been more available, instead of working on her dissertation every night. Then, after he wore out those excuses, the apologies came. The affair was all his fault. He was a fool. It would never happen again. *Let's go somewhere romantic to work things out*, Kyle had pleaded, and she'd agreed. But by the time they'd stepped off the plane in Venice, she'd known it was too late to make it work. *Too much water under the bridge*, she'd thought, not missing the irony that they'd landed in a city of canals.

Still, none of that mattered now. If she'd had a single lingering thought about giving their relationship another try, it had gone out the window the instant Mack carried her into her bedroom and gave her the best orgasm of her entire life.

"I doubt she'd care."

What? She'd almost forgotten Kyle was there. "But I thought you two were happy?" she asked, then wished she hadn't when his expression turned hopeful.

"It's not working, Gem. You know how I feel … " He shifted toward her, his hand reaching for hers.

She jumped to her feet, almost tripping on the coffee table in her rush to escape him. "Please don't do this now."

He followed her, stopping close, running a finger down her arm before taking her hands in his before she could back away. "I'm not giving up on us, you know. Can't you forgive me?"

"Aren't you forgetting something?"

He quirked his mouth up in that warm half-smile she'd always liked, although right now it had a lot less appeal beneath his pleading gaze. "I haven't forgotten a thing, my love. We were good together."

"I mean your girlfriend," she clarified patiently, pulling her hands from his. "The one living in your apartment."

Kyle's cheeks turned pink. "Oh, right. Actually, she's talking about moving out," he mumbled.

That had to hurt. Being ditched by the firm's junior intern would be pure hell for Kyle. The whole office would buzz over that one for weeks.

"I'm sorry," she said, although she didn't feel very sorry. Or glad. She just felt fed up with the situation.

"Look, why don't we—"

"Not now," Gemma snapped. "I'm sorry, I don't mean to be rude. I'm sorry things aren't working out with Miranda, and I'm sorry he went to your office." She crossed her arms in defense at his frown. "With everything that's going on, it's just too much at the moment."

Kyle stepped back, his frown replaced by surprise. "Well, the partners weren't impressed, that's for sure. Look, if Buchanan comes into the office again, I'll have to call the police. You do understand that I'll have no choice?"

Gemma nodded at the floor. "I *understand*."

"Does your mother know about this?"

Gemma's head flew up. Oh, hell. She'd completely forgotten about her mother. The last thing she needed was her mother on the doorstep, reproaching her that none of this would have happened if only she'd married Kyle. In her mom's mind, everything that went wrong—even the smallest thing—was always connected to her broken engagement.

"No, and she's not to know under any circumstances. Besides, she's on a cruise until next week."

Kyle grunted. "Under the circumstances, that's good. Right, we need to deal with this quickly, before it goes any further. Come into the office tomorrow, around four."

She nodded again, thankful to have at least some support. He might be her cheating ex, but right now he was her only lifeline. "I will. Thanks."

Kyle squeezed her hands. "And get some sleep. You look like hell."

Gemma forced a smile through her misery. "You're the second person to tell me that today."

She closed the door after him and poured herself a large glass of wine for comfort. Kyle was right. She needed to deal with the problem. Mack wasn't going to give up on this, so she might as well meet him head-on.

But how and where?

Then it hit her. She knew exactly what to do.

Walking through to the bedroom, she picked up his card, still lying on her nightstand, and pulled her phone from her bag. He answered after the second ring, but she didn't wait for him to speak.

"Mr. Buchanan. I'm ready to talk."

CHAPTER FIVE

No way was Dr. Gilmore ready to talk. Not in that tease of a dress and "do-me" shoes.

But at this exact moment in time, Mack couldn't say he was bothered about whether she uttered a single word. That short, low-cut pink sundress was bother enough. No sane man walking along Madison Avenue beside the mouthwatering Gemma Gilmore could ignore all that cleavage and the way her skirt flipped up around her thighs at every step. He damned well couldn't. Just looking at any part of her body was enough to heat him. Hell, why not just yank the sexy pink princess into a side alley and have his wicked way with her? Get it over and done with. Then talk.

Get a grip, Buchanan.

She stopped in the middle of the sidewalk. "We're here."

Where the hell was that, apart from Madison? "Here?"

"Yes, *here.* The Enright Museum of American Art—and my favorite place in the whole of New York," she explained with a sigh, starting up the steps of a brick building flanked by two massive columns. He almost tripped on his own feet as he followed, totally preoccupied with the sight of her hips swaying seductively in front of him. That had to be deliberate. She was good at it, for sure. Working her cute butt for all it was worth, her trim legs total perfection in hot-pink heels.

She turned, a small smirk playing at the sides of her mouth. Damn, she'd caught him staring. "Have you been to the Enright before?"

Mack paused, trying to shift his thoughts away from her legs by concentrating on not staring at her breasts. God, he was obvious.

"Can't say that I have." Frankly, he hadn't known the place existed. Not exactly his idea of a morning's entertainment.

She must have read his mind if the taunt in her eyes was anything to go by. "It exhibits fine art. I presume you know what fine art is?" She tilted her head toward the entrance. "Shall we?"

Okay, the princess had regained her confidence far more than he would have liked. She'd obviously worked through her options, made a plan, and in that dress, he could make a fairly decent guess what it involved. Lots of eye candy to distract him, followed by lots of questions about whom he worked for and how much he knew about the fraud. True, he couldn't ignore the fact that she was inconveniencing his libido, but he'd pretty much regained control since their last meeting, right? So her waggling her ass at him on the promise of more sack time wouldn't change anything. This wouldn't be so difficult.

He followed her into the lobby past a security guard, whose jaw dropped a foot at the sight sweeping past him. "Morning, Dr. Gilmore. You're paying us an early visit. We only opened two minutes ago."

"Hi, Bill," she chirruped brightly, her skirt bouncing high when she turned and aimed a brilliant smile in his direction. The poor guy was practically drooling when he winked at Mack.

"Right, Mr. Buchanan. Perhaps we should start with the seascapes. Something simple."

Time to get to the point. "Why are we here?"

She ignored his question. "Which artists do you like?"

He couldn't think of a single artist's name, let alone whether he liked them or not. But then she would've figured that. This was her turf, and her invitation to meet here was all about getting the upper hand by making him look ignorant. He got it. Not that he cared a rat's behind that she thought him a dumbass. He could play along until he was ready for some answers.

"What say you show me around?"

She smirked, and he started thinking about how good it would be to kiss that smug look right off her face.

"Right, Mr. Buchanan. Now if you actually *recognize* any artist's name, let me know and I'll explain their style." Her eyes rounded innocently. "Can you manage that?"

Ouch. "I'm all eyes and ears. After you."

She was still smirking as she led him through to the first exhibition room, her heels clicking briskly on the wood floor in time with her swinging skirt—all that leg, ass, and long, glossy ponytail right there in front of him. Sensational. Maybe this museum tour wouldn't be such a hardship after all.

She stopped, and he was so focused on her legs he almost fell over her. He could swear he heard her muffle a giggle. Yeah, she was having her fun.

She pointed at a painting. "This is by Edward Singer. Do you like it?"

Who? "It's okay."

She pouted, making her mouth look even more kissable. "'Okay' is not a term we use to appraise fine art. What do you *think* of it? You know, the composition, the use of color. Perhaps I should explain it to you?"

"I have a question."

Her head tilted in pretend interest. "Oh, really? What would you like to know?"

"Tell me about Kyle Lawrence."

That earned him a glare that could peel the paint clear off every canvas in the room. "You had no right to go to his office. He's got nothing to do with this."

She didn't look smug now. Just really pissed.

"I would've thought he had everything to do with this. He's your ex-fiancé, isn't he? You must have discussed it between ... screws." He paused, watching her blue eyes widen in shock and disgust as the words sank home. "The poor guy must have been all cut up when you called it off. No more of that luscious body of yours. Or am I wrong? You still see him, if I'm not mistaken."

For a second, he thought she was going to make for the exit, but surprisingly, she stood her ground. "You're unbelievably crude!"

"Yeah, my mother was always washing my mouth out with soap. Who's that by the way?" He walked over to study a bluish-colored painting of a couple standing on a beach, looking out to sea, except there was nothing to see but sea. What a waste of paint that was. "Boring if you ask me. Who did it?"

She still sounded sore. "Jackson Bell, you ignoramus."

He grinned and turned to meet her glare head on. She was as red as a ripe cherry, and darn if it didn't make her look all aroused and ready. Maybe they could fit in some sack time after all. He felt his cock thicken at the thought. Shit, an art tour with a hard-on. So much for getting a grip.

He nodded toward her left. "That one with the old shipwreck isn't bad. Who did that?"

She sighed. "Elizabeth Mannington."

"And the one next to it. The lighthouse painting?"

"Actually, that's a Frank Bonvalet."

"Yeah? Is it a fake?"

"Of course not, you—" She stopped, her professional pride getting the better of her prickles. Man, this was turning out to be the most fun he'd had in a long time. He'd never talked to a woman about art before. His dates usually involved dinner followed by a romp in the bedroom. Not that this counted as a date. But in some disconcerting way, he almost wished it was. He jettisoned the thought before it got traction. "It's the real deal then?"

She wrinkled her nose as if something unpleasant had settled under it. "Of *course*. I authenticated it."

"How do you know it's real?"

"What?"

"Tell me how you know it's a real Bonvalet." Not that he cared how she knew, but it would get them on track to discuss the forgery. Well, that was half-true. Mostly, he needed to get his mind off the tension in his jeans before it became obvious. "Come and explain it to me." He pointed to a spot on the floor directly in front of the painting. "Here."

From the look on her face, he might as well have asked her to stand in stinging nettles. "It wouldn't be possible to explain a masterpiece like that to you."

"Maybe I should come over there and get you. Interrogate you again." He kept his tone light but made the message clear: Fun or not, this was an investigation, he had a job to do, and he would get it done—amusing art tour or not.

She blinked at that, then with a shrug of resignation walked slowly over to him, but he could tell she wasn't about to concede.

"Well, I look at a whole range of things," she said, drawing the words out like she was explaining it to an imbecile. Leaning forward, she focused on a small section of the painting at the top-right corner, so he leaned in and focused as well, although all he could see were a lot of gray clouds and a few patches of reddish sky.

"Well, I'm listening, Sexy Legs."

His face was close enough to hear her soft intake of breath. He looked out of the corner of his eye, taking in the full, parted lips and dipped lashes. Jesus, was this just wishful thinking on his part, or was the good doctor actually turned on? The crasser his words, the more she seemed to like it.

Turned on or not, she recovered quickly. "Well, first, I look at the background of the work—where it came from, who owned it, the chain of sales. That's the first step in establishing the provenance." She paused, as if waiting for him to catch up. He should have felt insulted at that, but in truth, he was too busy eye-molesting every visible inch of her to do anything useful but nod.

"Got it. Go on."

"Then I look at whether the composition and style are consistent with the artist. The color of the primer and which paints were used and whether they match the period. The aging is important, of course. Paintings fade, and sometimes the paint cracks, so forgers will put those in the work, even matching their position exactly to the original if it hasn't been restored. Then there's the signature to authenticate. So you see, it covers all sorts of things."

"Oh yeah ... right." Not the swiftest response he'd ever made. "Are you sure it's not a fake? Looks pretty goddamn fake to me." That was mean. Playing with her.

Her spine shot straight. "God, you're an idiot!"

He grinned as she crossed her arms over her chest. It had the effect of plumping her breasts higher over the top of her sundress, distracting him all to hell again. But dammit if the princess didn't have the most appetizing rack. Yeah, he was a brute.

Her tone turned crisp. "Right, well, let's move on." She walked off, doing that thing with her hips again, turning her head to talk to him over her shoulder like he was some kid dragging his heels on a school trip. "Pick it up, Mr. Buchanan. There are lots of other works to see."

Mack stayed on the spot, rubbing the bridge of his nose and wondering how the hell he was going to play this. So far, all he'd managed to do was piss her off. She might look damned cute when she was mad, but it wasn't getting him very far.

She was already in the next room by the time he caught up. "So what would you like me to look at now?"

"Maybe these are more to your ... " She paused, sweeping a hand around the room, "*taste*. That is, if you've got any taste, which I doubt."

He glanced around and laughed. Hell, she might be looking down her nose at him, but at least this room didn't have sea pictures. It was a room full of nude women.

"Interesting."

"All by the same artist, Samuel Augustin. Do you like them?"

He looked closer. There had to be twenty paintings, all showing much the same thing. Women laying on couches, on rugs, a few standing by windows.

"The artist sure liked naked women." He watched her eyes narrow, no doubt waiting for something crude to come out of his mouth. He obliged.

"Did he fuck them all?"

Her eyes turned upward, as if in silent prayer. "The artist painted over sixty nudes during the 1920s and was arrested multiple times for exhibiting obscene images. So, what do you think?" Her tone went mocking. "Even you must be able to come up with something intelligent to say about nudes."

Mack walked over to a painting, pretending to show interest. Actually, it wasn't half-bad. A plump blonde lying on a red velvet couch, her long hair draped over a breast, one leg drawn up.

"It's passable, I guess."

She got that sneering tone again. "Is that all? Don't you get the essence of what the artist is saying? He's celebrating the beauty of the female form."

That sounded reasonable. He would happily celebrate the doctor's female form right now.

"Maybe we could explore the possibilities of you and me getting nude." Mack slid a step toward her, watching her eyes turn wary. "You know ... continue where we left off."

Her mouth sure did look kissable when it was hanging open in astonishment. "God, you're a philistine. I should have known better than to bring you here, you ignorant jerk."

He ignored her insult and carefully weighed his next steps. His strategy to tease her into opening up wasn't working. If anything, she had the upper hand.

He decided on a more direct approach.

"How long have you worked at McCallister's?"

She blinked in surprise. "What? Oh, for around seven years. Not that it's any of your business." She looked down and flexed her feet in her shoes, and Mack knew what that meant. All of a sudden, the doctor was nervous.

"And how many forgeries have you discovered?"

She snapped her head up at that, looking anxiously around the room as if the nudes could hear them. "I'm not discussing forgeries *here*. This is an art museum, after all."

He took two quick strides to stand directly in front of her. Her eyes shifted to the exit, probably estimating her chances of making an escape. He roughened his voice to take away that option. "You *will* talk to me about forgeries, Dr. Gilmore. Here or somewhere else, I don't care."

Surprisingly, she didn't quaver. She'd found a steeliness he hadn't reckoned on.

"You can't threaten me." She angled her head to look past him toward the door. "Besides, we have visitors, so I'm leaving."

Damn, she was right. An elderly couple was in the room, looking at the blonde on the couch. Mack put a hand under Gemma's elbow before she could move. "This way."

His touch got a reaction, but not half as much as he expected. Just a small tug of her elbow, more a token show of resistance than anything else. Maybe she was turned on again. The thought flipped around in his brain, sending blood to parts where he didn't need the extra help.

He steered her through the next two exhibition rooms, cursing that every room was occupied by at least one visitor. Didn't people have jobs to go to? There had to be somewhere they could talk. After walking her through another four exhibition areas, he finally found a small side room with no security camera.

"Start talking."

"What?"

"You know ... *talk*. That thing people do with their lips." He looked hard at her mouth. "Among other things."

She said nothing, so he took a step closer, which had her nervously sliding a step back. Her head turned, looking for an escape. "Remember, you called me, princess. Said you were ready to talk. So, talk."

"Who do you work for?"

"I get to ask the questions. Tell me when the Bonvalet arrived at McCallister's."

He thought she would try and push past him, but then she took a deep breath and answered, "Around seven weeks before the auction."

"And were you the first to see it?"

She shook her head. "No. Every work is recorded in McCallister's register first. The Bonvalet was unframed, so McCallister's mounted it in a temporary frame. It's a standard procedure. Can you at least tell me why you—"

He barked another question to keep her unsettled. "Where did you authenticate the Bonvalet?"

"In ... in my workroom at McCallister's. I worked on it during the day with a security guard present, and then he would take it away late afternoon to lock it in the safe."

"Who has access to the safe?"

"Maxim Stonebridge; John Allen, McCallister's operations manager; and the head auctioneer, who checks the works the day of the auction."

"So how long to authenticate the painting?"

"A few weeks, then it stayed in the safe until the day of the auction."

He already knew the answers to his questions. John had filled him in on every detail of the process. So far, she was telling the truth.

"How do you explain it being a fake?"

"I don't believe it's a fake. If I could have another look at it—"

"That's not going to happen." He shifted toward her, making her back up against the wall. She tried to look past him toward the doorway, so he moved to block her view. "No more games, Dr. Gilmore. The forger's name? Give me that, and I'll leave you alone." He made his tone brutal. Intimidating.

Her voice went weak, her eyes sliding away to stare at the exit. "I don't know any forger."

"Look at me. *Now.*"

Her gaze didn't shift from the exit, so he cupped her chin in his hand and tipped her head back to read her eyes. She was nervous all right, but it wasn't his questions that frightened her. It puzzled him, until her gaze moved to his mouth and her lips parted a fraction—then he knew. She wanted him. Right here, right now.

He'd been hanging on by a thread as it was, but that look sent his groin into overdrive within seconds. He closed his eyes, trying to quell the surging heat. It would be so easy to take her. Just lift her up, wrap her legs around his hips, slip her panties to one side ...

Fuck it, Buchanan, don't even think of it.

He could barely focus as he moved to stand only inches away, towering over her, hearing her breath hitch in response. Bracing one hand against the wall, he slipped the other around her small waist, pulling her flush to his hips, imprisoning her. Her small moan told him she could feel his erection against her belly, but as much as he liked the sound, there was something else he needed to do. He needed her to say the name. Bully it out of her, if that's what it took.

But he hadn't reckoned on his primal, protective urge toward this woman being so fierce—so gut-wrenching.

He dragged a breath and forced himself to say the words. "Stop fighting this, Gemma. It's over—can't you see that? I want you, and you want me. Just give me the name, and we can get past this damned charade."

Silence.

Damn his desire. *Do your fucking job, Buchanan.* "For God's sake, just give me the *name*!"

No name. No words of any kind. Just their raw lust for each other hanging thick in the air between them, everything they wanted just inches apart.

At that moment, he knew for certain she wouldn't talk. He'd questioned dozens of suspects in his intelligence career, knew when to push hard, when to play it soft. He'd thought she was the kind that broke easily. But this seemingly defenseless woman made him look like an amateur. She might even be innocent of the fraud, but he was long past making that call. His judgment was shot.

Mack made a decision. "Come with me."

Her eyes flashed confusion. "Where?"

He grabbed her hand and started pulling her toward the exit. "You'll see."

She hung back but didn't struggle. "What are you going to do?"

Mack didn't stop or look around. "Make love to you until neither of us can fucking walk."

CHAPTER SIX

Gemma wasn't sure where she was.

At the very least, she should find out. Then leave. But all she could think about were his words right before he'd towed her all the way back through the Enright and down the steps to a cab for the drive across town.

He was going to make love to her. *Love*, that's what he'd said. They would make love until they were too tired to walk. If Gemma had ever had a sexier thought, she didn't know what it was.

She hadn't even known this hotel existed, but it was six-star beautiful. Boutique-sized, exquisitely furnished, situated in an out-of-the-way cul-de-sac off a small Manhattan side street she hadn't known about. This couldn't be his room. There were no personal things lying around, or any sign at all that the room was occupied. Where he lived or stayed in New York was just another thing she didn't know about him. In fact, when she added up what she did know, it only came to two things: He was American and some kind of investigator. Not much, considering what they were about to do.

How all this had happened in the space of an hour was still beyond her. Admittedly, she had dressed in her prettiest, undeniably short sundress to get a reaction—but this? She'd only wanted to put him on her territory, distract him with the shortest dress in her closet, and then ask him questions about the fraud. That, and maybe tease him a little to get even. She should have known that playing with him would be dangerous. He'd seen her skimpy dress as nothing less than an invitation to take what he wanted. And as hard as she might try to convince herself otherwise, that's exactly why she'd worn it. But she really shouldn't be here. This could all be a carefully constructed plan on his part: play with her for a while, then interrogate her again once her defenses were down. But hell, he was the most exciting man she'd ever met, and that dangerous edge was all part of the whole alluring, irresistible package.

And what a package it was.

"Right, thanks." Mack took the keys from the porter and closed the door. Gemma shifted anxiously on her heels, focused on her breathing to stop herself from imagining every bone-melting thing he was about to do to her.

She watched him shrug off his jacket, trying not to be impressed by the way his powerful body flexed under his shirt and the superconfident way he moved as he tossed his jacket over the arm of the sofa. The man was beautiful, no doubt about it. Beautiful and dangerous.

He rolled his sleeve cuffs back, looking for all the world as if he was preparing to do business. The business being her, right now, going by the way his eyes were appreciating her from head to toe. If a stare could strip clothes off a body, she'd be in her birthday suit. Gemma tried, but failed, to tamp down the heat blossoming low in her belly. Dammit, she should *so* leave while she still had the strength.

"You need anything?" he asked, staring at her legs.

And the man was rude. Not even a show of good manners. No way was she going to just give in to him.

Gemma mustered up the haughtiest face she could find and gazed at a spot on the wallpaper.

He smiled quietly. "I guess that's a no."

He started walking toward her, so she took a step back, determined to maintain a decent distance. That wicked grin, and what it suggested, was positively indecent.

"What are you going to do?"

Stopping four feet from her, he stroked his jaw, as if working out the formalities of the situation. "How shall we do this?"

She took another step back. "Do what?"

Ignoring her question, he advanced again. "Perhaps a kiss to start things off."

Could a man really put *that* much sexy promise in a statement?

"A kiss," she echoed stupidly, shaking her head, but at the same time hoping he would just do it. She was starting to feel dizzy with sexual heat or nerves or something.

He took a single stride to reach her, slipped an arm around her waist, and—before she could attempt a protest—turned her face up and his mouth was on hers.

So much for her exit plan. She whispered against his lips, "Mack."

He lifted his head in surprise. "That's the first time you've said that. I like it."

Although Gemma didn't want to admit to herself that there was anything remotely likable about this man, she liked it, too. In fact, she loved the sound of his name on her lips. Mack. It suited him. Big, like a Mack truck. An unbelievably sexy truck. Powerful, intense, rough, but at the same time gentle.

He cupped a hand around the back of her neck to hold her head steady as he kissed her again, this time his tongue taking over her mouth, demanding every last bit of her attention. Gemma tried hard not to like it so much, but she couldn't help it. Only a couple of kisses in, and here she was, kissing him back, pushing her own tongue greedily into his mouth, her body responding to the low growl of approval rising from deep in his throat.

His mouth was still on hers when his hand dropped from her waist to pull up her dress and ease his hand inside her panties. No time-wasting. Straight into it, taking what he wanted. She shivered as his fingers spread across her butt, his hand so broad that it covered most of her backside. She barely had time to think about what was coming next before he'd released her mouth to ease her back a fraction. Expecting him to pick her up and carry her to the bed, Gemma lifted an arm, ready to loop it around his neck. But then, with a soft laugh, he slid his hand around her hip to brush his fingers over her sex.

"Open your legs."

She blinked in surprise but obeyed him, trying to stop her heels from wobbling as she widened her stance. Maybe he wanted her legs wide so he could wrap them around his hips when he carried her to the bed.

But he didn't do any of that. Very slowly, he slid two fingers lightly along her, repeating the process until she was squirming hungrily. It wasn't even close to enough, and he had to know that she needed more.

"Please ... the bed." Gemma knew she was begging, but she was past caring.

But he didn't pick her up or even let her find her own way. His fingers just stayed light and busy on her, before stopping briefly. Now what? Then he started again, this time exploring more carefully, using his fingers to spread her open.

Moments later he found her clit.

He was going to make her come right here, standing up.

Surely he didn't really expect her to stay upright with his fingers stroking and teasing at her like that? The man was cruel.

Cruel or not, she still gripped his big hand to hold it steady against herself, not caring when a soft laugh rumbled above her head. If he was having his fun with her, too bad. No way was she about to let go. Right now, her whole world was that small, tight bud of a million nerve endings about to explode into one mind-blowing orgasm, and his thumb was going to get her there.

She was at the edge, just a few more strokes ...

He stopped.

Oh God, he's going to leave me hanging.

Gemma dug her fingernails into his hand in protest, terrified that he was done with her. Not even he could be so merciless.

His mouth brushed lightly over her ear.

"Open your legs wider."

Oh, sweet mercy, that erotic command alone almost made her climax without further help. Gripping two fistfuls of his shirt for stability, she spread her legs as wide as was safe in five-inch heels, leaned forward to rest her face against his chest, and silently prayed for relief.

"Good." She didn't know whether it was a question or a confirmation resonating from above, but it didn't matter. A second later, he dipped down and two fingers slid deep inside her body. Gemma scrunched her eyes shut, sinking into the intense sensation of his fingers slowly pumping her, his thumb making beautiful circles over her clit.

The man knew how to tease and torture, taking her to the brink, then backing off before building again, each stimulation more powerful than the last, until Gemma thought she would pass out from sheer lust.

Then finally, when he knew she couldn't stand it for another moment, he let her come, tightening his hold around her waist as she arched back over his arm, almost sobbing with gratitude. At that point, her entire body shuddered helplessly in unison with every thick, pulsating wave that radiated out from her core, over and over, the strength of it making her cry out. She'd thought the orgasm he'd given her two days ago was the best of her entire life. That was then. This had just put her on another planet.

Her eyes were still closed when she felt his breath on her cheek.

"I take it that hit the spot."

Gemma tried to laugh, but it came out as a kind of wheeze. He chuckled, lifting her up and carrying her to the bed to lay her down. His voice dropped to a heat-sizzling growl that had her wriggling in anticipation.

"Right, now we get started."

Then he stripped.

Even her wildly vivid fantasies of him naked fell a mountain short. The man was constructed of nothing but brute strength. In her apartment, she hadn't really had the chance to study him, but now she could absorb every glorious inch of pure masculine beauty. Many glorious inches, standing thick and proud.

There were scars on him as well. A three-inch silver-colored scar across his shoulder, a small crescent-shaped mark on his arm that could be an old bullet wound, and a long, jagged red scar down his side that looked recent. Everything about him confirmed her initial impression. Whatever his job, that supermuscular physique served as a work tool. He occupied a world where strength and self-control were vital to survival.

He settled down beside her, plucking at a thin shoulder strap of her sundress, frowning as if he didn't know what to do with it. She giggled.

He looked so serious she giggled again.

"What are you laughing at, woman? This needs to come off."

Obediently she sat up and slid the zipper down, taking it slow, wanting to tease. Her dress had barely slipped from her breasts when she couldn't go on, totally distracted as he lightly thumbed a nipple.

"Keep going."

"Heels?" Lord, she felt wanton.

He grunted. "On."

She wriggled out of the dress and panties before falling back on the bed. Waiting.

His gaze traveled the length of her.

Gemma couldn't recall ever feeling so scrutinized. Or so turned on by a stare. Nor could she wait to touch him. Taking the lead, she kissed her way down his chest, feeling his fingers pulling at the tie holding her ponytail.

Her hair was loose around her shoulders by the time she'd slipped all the way down to flick her tongue over the head of his cock, tasting him. She heard him catch his breath in surprise. Oh, she was so going to return the favor.

She closed her lips around the broad head, feeling him shudder in her mouth. Yes, she was doing it right. She took more of him, gently laving and sucking, her hand holding his shaft steady to her mouth. He shuddered harder, his hand fisting her hair.

"Christ."

"You're so hard," she breathed against him before lifting her head to peek up at his face through her lashes, her hand taking over for her mouth. His shaft was warm and silky and so big her fingers didn't quite meet around him.

He took a while to answer. "I feel fucking hard."

Then she took as much of him as she could fit in her mouth, using her tongue to caress his length with every slide upward before dipping deep again. He moaned, his fingers gripping her hair harder now, as if to hold her in place. Gemma repeated her slow movements over and over, enjoying every fresh moan of his pleasure when she dipped deep. She was giving herself pleasure too—he tasted so good. She could totally do this forever, but he was close, and she wouldn't tease him like he had her.

She had only just increased her pace when—in one easy movement—he bent down, lifted her up, and sat her on top of him. Just like that. As if she weighed nothing more than a six-week-old kitten.

"Hey, I was enjoying that."

"Come here," he growled with a laugh, hooking a hand around the back of her head and pulling her hard to his mouth. Gemma promptly forgot about everything except for his tongue stroking the inside of her mouth and his hands taking complete charge of her body.

He eased her back, angling his head in the direction of the bedside table. "My wallet."

"What?"

"Condom."

"Oh." She reached over and picked up the leather wallet, fighting the temptation to even glance at it in case he thought she was prying. Besides, he was watching her, maybe even waiting for her to sneak a look. She held it toward him.

"Here."

"You do it."

Gemma blinked. Had he just asked her to look in his wallet?

"Are you sure?"

He lifted an eyebrow. "I'm not some fucking James Bond with an exploding wallet. Get the condom."

That might have been funny if she hadn't been so desperate for him. The first compartment had what she was looking for. *Five*? Oh, sweet Lord, he really did come prepared.

He tore the wrapper and fitted the sheath superfast, while Gemma looked on in desire and fascination. His every movement was ultrasmooth and precise. The man was a like a beautiful, well-oiled machine. Maybe he really was a James Bond.

She felt cheeky. "Can I be on top, James?"

He flipped her on her back to settle his big body between her legs. Holding himself up on his elbows, he half-smiled down at her. "Later, Blue Eyes. Put your legs around me."

Now she felt really cheeky. "God, you're so bossy."

His smile turned to a throaty laugh as he slipped a hand under a calf to wrap it up around his hip, then did the same with the other. Her hot-pink heels rested on his butt. "And don't you love it?"

"I do not!" she protested. Actually, she did. Not that she was going to admit that to him.

He kissed her, and moments later he was inside her body, sliding his length to the very end of her in one long, deep thrust. She gasped at the sheer invasion of it, feeling her core stretched wide as he merged his body with hers, drowning her in a sea of sensation. Hot. Thick. The most erotic feeling of being taken by a man who knew exactly how to take a woman.

"You feel so good," he groaned into her hair. She could only moan her response as his hand went under her butt to fasten her hips to his. He held still for the briefest moment, then, slowly, he began to move, working himself in and out of her body, almost leaving her completely as he withdrew and then sliding home again in one long, easy stroke.

Oh sweet paradise, how he took his time with her, getting to know what she liked better than she knew herself. Deep, powerful thrusts that had her sobbing for release, then whimpering with pleasure when he eased off, delaying her orgasm. Gemma knew, without a shadow of a doubt, that this was what it was supposed to be like. She'd never felt so alive in her entire life. This wasn't just sex. He was making love to her. A man she didn't even know and would probably never know.

"Oh God, that's so good, I … love … " The word escaped from Gemma's mouth before she could stop it, suddenly terrified he would misinterpret what she'd said. But seconds later, she forgot it entirely as he angled his head to reach her mouth for a long, deep, incredibly tender kiss. Then moments later, knowing that they were both ready, he drove piston-fast into her, driving them toward climax. She felt her hips lifted high off the bed for more penetration, his arm braced on the mattress, holding them both up.

Her orgasm came in one huge burst of ecstasy—powerful contractions that made her cry out as wave after wave crested along every nerve in her body, their force peaking right at the moment when she felt him pulsate his release into her core.

He didn't let her go. Rolling over onto his side, he took her with him so they were still joined, their bodies covered in a sheen of perspiration. Gemma settled herself into his big shoulder. He might never tell her who he was or whom he worked for, but right now she had this moment of utter contentment.

"A pity," he murmured against the top of her head. He sounded serious.

Her head sprang up in alarm. "What's wrong?"

"You didn't have a turn on top."

She sighed and dropped back into his shoulder. "Yes, it was disappointing."

His chin nuzzled her hair. "Perhaps I can ease your disappointment."

"Oh, how would you do that?"

He didn't answer. Instead he rolled out of her, dealt with the condom, and shoved himself off the bed. "Lose the shoes."

So bossy. But more importantly, what was he planning? Whatever it was, he was almost fully erect again. She kicked off her stilettos, sending them over the side of the bed, shivering as his hazel eyes grazed every inch of her while he fitted a fresh condom and lifted her into his arms. "You'll see."

Whatever he had in mind, at least it didn't involve her having to stand. He carried her through to the bathroom, his eyes locked on hers.

"Ever fucked in the shower?"

The man was so to the point; it was like being immersed in some incredibly erotic language. An ache dug deep at the apex of her thighs.

"No." She gulped, barely able to imagine what was coming. She and Kyle had tried to have shower sex a few times, but Kyle preferred the comfort of a bed, so that's where they had always ended up. His bed, of course, as hers was too small.

He held her effortlessly with one arm as he tossed the spare condom on a shelf and turned on the spray. Steam quickly rose around them, fogging up the glass of the huge walk-in shower.

"Hang onto me."

He backed her up against the tiles of the shower wall, one hand around her waist, the other below her, rubbing his cock against her opening before slowly inching the head into her. "Okay?"

She jerked a nod into his shoulder and tightened her hold around his neck as he entered her, the sensation bowing her back as he slid home, anchoring her to his body. Then he stilled, and they both savored the rush of water running over their wet bodies and the steam enveloping them in a warm, wet blanket. Gemma leaned her head back against the tiles and closed her eyes, loving the feeling of being filled to completeness by this dangerous man who gave her raw, sensual pleasure like she'd never known it.

Her eyes were still closed when, slowly, he began to move inside her, taking his time to build a steady tempo, each stroke pushing her up the slippery wall, his arms securing her hips to his.

He was doing all the work: she wanted to help, but he was in total command, leaving her helpless under his powerful thrusts. When he pulled back to look down at her breasts, she could feel them bounce with every drive upward.

"Beautiful," he grinned, jiggling her in his arms to make them bounce harder.

Oh God, the man was so sexy.

"You're close," he whispered into her mouth when he kissed her, but Gemma no longer had the strength to speak. Her whole body was jelly, the warm water made exquisite sensations on her tight nipples, and he was inside her, taking her higher and higher ...

Then she was there again—one big upward spiral of gratification. Through her climax, she could feel him move his knee under her, bracing himself against the wall for leverage as he surged harder into her moments before his release.

When they finally regained their breathing, he leaned down to kiss her lightly.

"Fucking good, isn't it?"

Gemma sighed contentedly. Fucking fantastic more like it.

•••

The man certainly lived up to his promises. Gemma literally felt weak at the knees from sex. And she'd had a turn on top.

This was so not how she'd planned to spend her day, although for the life of her, she couldn't exactly remember what the plan had been, except there had been one. The Enright and—oh, hell, that's right—to meet Kyle at four.

Okay, she could still make it. He was back in the shower, her hair was dried off, and she was mostly dressed. All she had to do was find her panties, wherever they were.

The shower was still running when she finally dragged them from under the bed.

But there was a distraction. Try as she might to ignore it, it was just sitting there, tempting her like a pair of Jimmy Choo pumps in a January sale.

His wallet.

Turning her head, she listened. The water was still running.

Of course, she shouldn't do it. But, she reasoned, she knew nothing about him and needed to know at least *something*. Otherwise, how could she ever clear her name? Besides, there might be one or two useful things to tell Kyle when she met him. But still, it didn't seem right. He'd made love to her, and she'd loved him right back. For hours.

For a long moment, she hesitated.

Should she do this?

Yes, she should. Flicking open the wallet, she checked the compartments. She found a generous amount of cash, but no driver's license, registration, or even a credit card. Understandable, if he were James Bond. But just as she was about to give up, she noticed the corner of a folded piece of paper protruding from a small side compartment. Easing it out a fraction, she paused again to listen. Safe. He was still in the shower.

Four rows of three numbers, nothing else.

Whatever they were, they were all she had. Gemma scanned the rows, chanting each line under her breath before closing her eyes to visualize them. There was only enough time to repeat the process once before she heard the water turn off and she had to slip the paper back where she found it.

But by then she had every row memorized.

CHAPTER SEVEN

"She took the bait."

"You think it'll work?"

Mack lowered his phone and closed his eyes, wishing he didn't have to do this. Hell, what was wrong with him? This was nothing special. Just a simple assignment to keep him occupied until he went back in the field.

"Mack, are you still there?"

"Yeah, I'm here. It'll work. She's a smart girl. Smart enough to memorize a set of numbers in less than thirty seconds. She'll figure it out."

"And do you still think she's involved? If McCallister's says the Bonvalet is a perfect copy, maybe she was really fooled."

"McCallister's doesn't believe it was an honest mistake. From what the operations manager, John Allen, says, there are only three authenticators in the world with her knowledge of Bonvalet, and she's considered the best. If she worked with an expert forger, no one would ever know the fake from the real thing. And remember, nobody had seen it for forty years."

"So next steps?"

"Allen will contact her and set up a meeting at McCallister's. From there, we just wait and see what she does."

"Right. We've had no luck with identifying the forger—all we know is he's still in Venice. We have two guys on it full time, but it won't be easy to track him down. We need her to talk."

He sighed. "She's a lot tougher than I first thought. Anyway, I'll be in touch as soon as it's over."

He ended the call and sat on the end of the bed, brooding.

He hadn't wanted to set a trap but there it was. A spur-of-the-moment decision to slip the numbers into his wallet while she was in the bathroom drying off her hair. He half-hoped it wouldn't work, but he had to give it a try. To have any chance of connecting her to the fraud, she needed to be caught red-handed.

But was she guilty? Despite all his questioning, she'd never once wavered. But then maybe she's just very clever at playing innocent. Either way, all they could do was wait. After meeting with Allen, her actions would probably confirm her involvement in the fraud, and she could be arrested. After that, Mack's part in the investigation would be over.

Investigation. Yeah, he'd investigated her all right. To the point where he now knew every inch of her. She was beautiful. And smart. And in his head. Even if, by some miracle, she was actually genuinely fooled by the fake painting, he still couldn't take things further. Relationships didn't fit on his radar. His work was dangerous by even the toughest undercover intel standards. His last job had almost killed him. A stupid mistake on his part. But if nothing else, it served as a brutal reminder of why he stuck to a solo life.

He slipped on his jacket and grabbed the room pass, looking across to the bed, smiling wryly at the wreckage of bed linens. But man, they'd been hot for each other. He could have had her again if she hadn't taken off, saying she had an appointment. It had to be her ex, Kyle Lawrence. She'd be looking for legal advice no doubt. Maybe something more. Damn, he shouldn't care.

He closed the hotel door and walked to the elevator, trying to ignore the heaviness in his chest. He *did* care about Gemma Gilmore. Far too much.

Don't sweat it, Buchanan. It's just a job.

He just needed to believe it.

• • •

"You want coffee?"

"No thanks. You've gotten a bigger office. Nice view."

"The perks of senior partnership. You're flushed," Kyle said, almost accusingly.

For one horrible moment, she thought Kyle had figured out the reason. She was so full-on post-orgasmic her body was still humming.

"Oh, it's nothing," she fibbed, looking around the room in a desperate attempt to avoid Kyle's inquisitive attorney gaze. "It was a rush to get here on time."

It was true enough. Running late, and afraid that Mack would distract her into forgetting the numbers, she'd gabbled something about an appointment and then practically bolted from the hotel room, leaving him standing naked in the bathroom doorway with a towel slung over his shoulder. It was all she could do not to throw herself at him and beg him to make love to her again.

"Is that a new dress?"

Gemma started. He still sounded accusing. "Oh, just something summery I picked up," she said a little breathlessly.

He looked it over and frowned. "There's not much of it. Right, so about Mack Buchanan. Where did you first meet him?"

This was tricky. There really wasn't an easy way to say *I tried to pick him up* without sounding desperate. Not only would her upstanding ex consider it "unbecoming," he'd think her a total dimwit, considering all that had happened in the past two days.

"He was at McCallister's the day the Bonvalet sold."

"Go on."

"We were in the same area of the auction room."

"Go on."

"One of us made a comment about the auction. I don't remember who it was."

"And ... "

She shrugged, faking nonchalance. "There's nothing more to tell. We watched the auction."

Kyle leaned forward and drummed his fingers impatiently on the desk.

"Gem, if we're going to get anywhere with this, you have to tell me everything. You understand? *Everything*."

"Everything?" she echoed, feeling her cheeks going pink all over again under Kyle's probing stare. She'd definitely leave out a few details, although he was now looking at her suspiciously. Did she have "multiple orgasms" emblazoned on her forehead or something?

"Somehow we got into a conversation about art," she said on a rush. "He asked if I liked the Bonvalet, that's all. After the sale, I left."

"And the next time you saw him?"

"In Maxim Stonebridge's office, when Maxim told me about the forgery. I ... fainted and Mack Buchanan took me home." Crap. She shouldn't have said that. Kyle's eyebrows had flown up. "Actually, he insisted on coming in ... "

Oh, hell. Now she'd done it.

Kyle's eyebrows went higher. "You let him into your apartment? For Christ's sake, Gem."

"I didn't have a choice. He forced his way in." She squirmed in her chair, trying to quell the heat in her cheeks. "You know what he's like," she finished lamely.

"Jesus, you should have called the police. That guy seems capable of anything."

Capable didn't begin to describe it. For most of the morning, Mack had demonstrated his capability. She shook off the sizzling thought as more unwanted warmth flooded her face. "Anyway, there's not much else to tell. I met Lucy yesterday afternoon, and she's going to get my Bonvalet notes and photos."

Except Lucy hadn't texted or called, which was strange. Knowing Lucy's nosiness and enthusiasm for missions, she would've gone straight to the workroom upon arriving at the office—right about the time when Gemma and Mack were at the Enright. But her phone hadn't buzzed once all day, and there was no point in calling Lucy if the girl didn't have any news.

"How long did he stay?"

"Not long," she mumbled absently, looking down to adjust the strap of her purse as a distraction. Dammit, Kyle wasn't going to let this go. "He just asked a lot of questions about who the forger was, that's all."

She looked up to find Kyle's brown eyes fixed on hers like a set of crosshairs. "*And ...* what else?"

Gemma found herself chewing at her lip, then realized with a start that Kyle was staring at her mouth. He knew her so well he could read the message it sent: guilt. She released it fast.

"He said something about other agencies coming after me, such as the FBI."

"Anyone else?"

Kyle was almost as dangerous as Mack when it came to interrogation. Not surprising, considering his formidable skill at questioning witnesses on the stand.

"Not that I can remember."

To her relief, he seemed satisfied with her answer, at least for the moment. "So, at this stage, no one else has spoken to you about the fraud. You've not been contacted by the police or any federal agency?"

"No. What do you think it means?"

Kyle shrugged and relaxed back in his chair. "Going by what's happened, Buchanan's just guessing. If he had proof of your involvement, the police would have arrested you by now. After you authenticated the work, you never saw it again. There's no direct connection."

"The thing is, Per—I mean Mack Buchanan won't even say who he works for." She chewed her lip again while she thought, not caring that Kyle was watching. "I still don't understand why they think it was me."

"Was it?"

"*Kyle!*"

"Don't get mad." His mouth quirked up in a grin. "It helps to know guilt or innocence before representation."

Oh. She hadn't even thought of that. It seemed so drastic. "Will I need representation?"

Kyle stood and came around his desk, sat on a corner, and stared down at her bare thighs. "Probably." He shrugged. "But don't worry about it. I'll set up a meeting with McCallister's in a few days. They have no proof of your involvement, so they'll have to reinstate you. If they don't, we sue. Just a hint of bad publicity will destroy their reputation, so they'll fold. Or, they might offer you a hefty settlement to resign. Either way, you'll be fine."

Fine? She didn't want fine. She wanted her old life and reputation back.

"It sounds so cold. McCallister's was—is—my whole life."

"What about dinner tonight?"

She didn't much like this new direction.

"What for?"

She was being rude, but it didn't stop Kyle leaning down to take her hand. "Hey, let me take you to dinner." He flashed a smile. "You know how I feel. Just give us a chance to talk things through, that's all I ask." She tamped down the instinct to pull her hand away. Kyle had loved her, and she'd loved him. Maybe not as much as she should have, and maybe there hadn't been the sexual sparks that made her body sing the way she would have liked, but that wasn't everything. They had been happy together. And truthfully, she *had* neglected him for months, working on her dissertation when she could have been enjoying her engagement and planning her dream wedding. Okay, he'd cheated with Miranda, but she could deal. Lots of people cheat, and their partners get past it, right?

Wrong.

Gemma tugged her hand free. "There's nothing to talk about, Kyle. You made your choice." Needing to segue to something more pressing, she dug into her purse, pulling out her phone. "By the way, I have a set of numbers." She held the phone to him. "I've no idea what it means, but could it be a Swiss bank account number or something?"

Kyle's brow furrowed as he studied the rows of numbers on the screen. "No, too short for a bank account number, but ... hang on, it looks like it could be a combination."

"You mean to a bank deposit box?"

He shook his head. "No, a safe."

"Are you sure?" She stared at the rows again.

"Yeah, that's how safe combinations are usually written. Where'd you get them?"

How to word this?

"I came across them in an old file in my workroom." She shoved the phone back in her bag and pretended to search for a tissue.

Of course he knew she was lying. She had to look like a guilty defendant sitting in the witness box. Why on earth hadn't she kept her mouth shut?

"How did really you get them, Gem?"

She tried to empty her mind of the hotel room, but she could feel the guilty heat seeping into every pore of her cheeks. "Um ... like I said, they were in a file."

Kyle's voice rose in irritation. "You noted them for a reason. Tell me."

She might as well just fess up and get it over with.

"I stole them from Mack Buchanan's wallet, all right?" She winced. That sounded so bad.

Kyle's face grew red splotches as he stood up and glared down at her short dress. Standing beside her, he seemed almost intimidating, but maybe she'd just never seen him so worked up before.

"How the *hell* did you get access to his wallet?"

She was so screwed.

"Oh, it was nothing," she answered vaguely, desperately wanting to claw back the last minute.

"You've been with him!"

It wasn't so much a question as an angry accusation, but she answered anyway. "It's not what you think." Lord, could a set of words sound more guilty?

"Oh, Jesus. Where?"

Closing her eyes, Gemma prayed for strength to say the words. Kyle would stay on this like a dog with a bone until she told him everything. Besides, if she didn't tell him, he'd probably call Mack and find out for himself. Worse, he'd spill the beans to Kyle on every sordid detail.

"A hotel," she blurted. Why did that sound so cheap?

"*When?*"

Gemma tried to make her voice sound normal, but it came out as a squeak. "Today." Oh, it was so much worse than cheap. It was downright tawdry. Sliding her eyes to the side, she saw Kyle take a step back, as if she physically repulsed him.

Looking up, she didn't think she'd ever seen Kyle so flushed.

"You *fucked* him before coming here? The guy who's trying to ruin your whole career? You want me to give you legal advice about the man you've just been with?"

His outrage slammed at her conscience so brutally she felt dizzy. How to explain? That it just happened. That she was a fool. That she'd never see Mack again. Oh, dear God, those were the exact excuses Kyle had given *her* when she'd found out about Miranda.

"I'm sorry, Kyle. I know it looks bad. I never meant ... " She closed her mouth, knowing there was nothing to say that would lessen his anger and hurt. Any excuse would sound pathetic. And she'd hurt the one person who was trying to help her. Of course, after what Kyle had done, she owed him nothing. It wasn't as if they were still together, even if he still wanted to think so.

He sat down and slumped back, shaking his head in disbelief. "How did it happen?"

Good question. The whole thing had been a blur from start to finish.

"I met him at the Enright this morning. Just to try and get some information about who he works for, that's all. It was stupid, I know. But he ... well, he ... "

Kyle's eyes drilled hers as he leaned forward in his chair. "What?"

"He asked me questions about the forgery, and when I couldn't tell him anything, he took me to a hotel," she answered, pulling at the hem of her dress as if that could, somehow, stretch it to a decent length. She didn't even have to look up to know that Kyle was disgusted. She could practically taste it coming at her from across his desk.

"And you went with him? Good God, have you no sense? Didn't you think it strange, under the circumstances? Christ, Gem, the guy's dangerous. You're not dealing with some bumbling, overweight private investigator going around photographing cheating spouses. From the look of him, he must be military intelligence or something close to that. The fact that he's even been brought in on this case should be warning enough that there's a lot more to this whole thing."

He shook his head again in disbelief. "It's so unlike you to do something like this. And if McCallister's finds out, that could be the end of you ever working for them again. Apart from being incredibly sordid, it's ... well, it's *unprofessional*."

The censure lifted her hackles. Okay, going to a hotel with an almost-stranger might not be her smartest move, but there was no need to make a federal case out of it. And no way would she tolerate him questioning her professionalism. Kyle could get off his moral high horse right now.

She put on her best pout. "That's not fair! What happened *happened*, and it's done with. I won't be seeing him again, so there's no point in discussing it."

But she didn't really believe her words, and from Kyle's resentful expression, he didn't either. Mack would be back, bringing his hot body with him. She still wanted him. Lord, she so needed to have her self-preservation instincts professionally examined.

Gemma jumped to her feet, suddenly longing for the solitude of her apartment. "Is there anything else you should know before I leave?"

He sighed and followed her to the door. "No, but I'll set up a time with McCallister's." He took her arm and turned her around to face him. "Does Buchanan know you have the numbers?"

She shook her head. "No, he was in the shower."

He had that disgusted look again. "Look, if anyone contacts you about the fraud, tell them you're only talking through your lawyer. Can you at least manage that?"

She nodded.

"And for God's sake, stay away from Buchanan. I mean it, Gem. This is serious."

She nodded again and left him raking his fingers through his fair hair. He was hurting. Jealous. Worried for her.

She had almost reached the elevator when her phone rang. Lucy's name glowed on the screen. Wonderful Lucy.

"Hey Lucy. I've been waiting to hear from you."

"You'll never believe it, GG. You just so totally *won't* believe it!"

Gemma scrunched her eyes shut, holding her breath, waiting for the glorious news that would give her something to think about other than her disastrous meeting with Kyle.

"What won't I believe, sweetie?"

"Jamie and I went on a date. A *real* date, not just for a burger or anything like that. First he took me to dinner—"

Hell! If she could murder someone by just thinking it, that girl would be toast.

"*Lucy!*" she interrupted, trying hard to control her exasperation. The last thing she needed was her best detective hanging up in a huff. "The notes, girl. The notes."

"Sorry, GG. They're gone."

Gemma closed her eyes, willing her tone to calmness. "What do you mean, *gone*?"

"Gone. Jamie went through every cabinet in your workroom. Nada."

Gemma leaned against the wall, suddenly feeling weak. "Have you any idea who has them?"

"No, and it's so annoying because usually I know these things."

Annoying all right. The one thing she really needed, and Lucy was stumped. That could only mean one thing.

Mack Buchanan.

He had her notes. It was only logical: If any of her coworkers in the office had taken them, Lucy would know who it was. Damn him.

"Do you want me to find out who has them? It might take a while, but I'm sure I can find out."

"Sure, Lucy." Gemma didn't hold out much hope, but still, Lucy might get lucky. Knowing for sure that Mack had her notes wouldn't make much difference, but at least it would give her something to go on. "Anyway, how are things at the office?"

"Okay, I guess. You know, old grumpy-chops Allen called a staff meeting this morning. He says McCallister's security system is down for a few days, so all afterhours access to the building has been stopped. It's like Fort Knox around here. You know, Jamie just loves sailing, and his father has a yacht. We're going out on Saturday. And you know, GG, he's *so* good at kissing."

Gemma couldn't help but smile at Lucy's description of John Allen. It was pretty close to accurate, even if John was only forty. In Lucy's teenage brain, anyone a day past thirty was ancient. "That's nice. Listen, sweetie, I have to go, but keep in touch, won't you?"

"Veronica Mars is on the job. See ya." Lucy giggled.

Gemma arrived home an hour later, her floaty, post-orgasmic state totally gone. All she had now was a blazing headache. She needed sleep. Taking two acetaminophen, she fell into bed.

Five minutes later, her phone buzzed. It was old grumpy-chops himself.

"Can you come into the office tomorrow, Dr. Gilmore? There are a few things I need to discuss with you."

She didn't feel particularly obliging toward the hard-nosed John Allen.

"That's not possible. Can't you tell me now?"

He ignored her cool tone. "This needs to be discussed in person. What say we make it late tomorrow afternoon, around six?"

What say she hung up on him? Except McCallister's might have realized their mistake and wanted to apologize. An invitation to meet at the office should make her feel better, but somehow it only gave her a sense of foreboding.

"All right. I'll see you at six."

Ending the call, she sank back into her pillows. Overall, it had been an up-and-down day. In more ways than one.

CHAPTER EIGHT

It felt strange to be back at McCallister's. Only a few days ago, she'd been dragged out of the place like a criminal who'd committed the crime of the century. She half-expected to see an FBI wanted poster of herself on the wall of John Allen's office.

"Please take a seat, Dr. Gilmore."

So typical of John. Always formal and polite, but cold. Today he was in his usual steel-gray suit and steel-gray tie, looking his usual steely, composed, unemotional self. If he had good news for her, it obviously didn't include the words *welcome back*.

Gemma sat down in the chair opposite his desk, now wishing she hadn't come. For a start, she didn't like the way he was looking at her—like she was a naughty schoolgirl brought in front of the principal for reprimanding. And now he was ignoring her by shuffling through his papers while she sat waiting. So rude. If he didn't say something soon, she'd get up and go find a coffee.

Two impatient, toe-tapping minutes later, he finally looked up and paid attention to her, his voice crisp.

"Right, Dr. Gilmore." He paused to glance disapprovingly over her dress jeans and blue silk shirt as if she'd come to school out of uniform. "We have progressed on uncovering the fraud." He waited for a response, but she stayed silent, deciding then and there that if he intended to pause like that between every sentence, she'd definitely go find that coffee.

"Philip Taurel has agreed to have the painting examined. It was delivered here yesterday."

She sat up, her irritation dissipated. Progress at last. Now she could finally clear this whole thing up.

"I'm so pleased that you have it, John. Can I see it now—to check its authenticity?"

He shook his head, and she caught the hard flicker of satisfaction in his eyes. Drat John Allen. She'd always had the impression that he resented her success, but even so, she hadn't expected the man to take such blatant pleasure from her fall from grace.

"You won't be *checking* the painting. It will be examined by a forensic investigator employed by Mr. Taurel. Our insurers insisted the painting be examined at McCallister's with a representative from the insurance company present."

Okay, so she wouldn't perform the examination, but that didn't really matter. Philip Taurel's expert would establish that it was genuine.

"Can I at least be there when it's examined?"

He looked at her as if she'd just asked him for a Lamborghini. "Of course *not!* We also have your notes."

Going by his smug expression, her surprise must have been obvious.

"So it was you who took my notes ... " Her voice died when he shook his head.

"Actually it was Mr. Buchanan who retrieved them from your workroom."

"I need to see them, John. That's the only way I can—"

He shook his head impatiently. "He also informed us that Lucy Barton and Jamie O'Mara had gone through your filing cabinets. They will, of course, be investigated. If we find that either of them helped you with the fraud, both will be referred to the police."

"Oh no, they weren't helping—" Gemma stopped. That sounded halfway to a confession.

"It's all over, *doctor*." He spat the last word in a self-satisfied bark.

"What do you mean?" Gemma couldn't stop her voice from trembling—which seemed to please John Allen no end. He might resent her, but even so, she hadn't expected such outright hostility from him.

"Of course, once the investigator compares your notes to the forgery, it will be obvious that you knew."

"I don't know—"

He carried on as if she hadn't spoken. "Of course, it's your notes. They won't match the painting. That discrepancy alone will be enough to convict you."

Going by his smirk, her shocked gasp was exactly the sound he wanted to hear.

"For goodness' sake, John," she flashed impatiently, "I didn't deliberately authenticate a forgery. In fact, the notes will prove the painting I saw was genuine."

There was no mistaking the icy gleam of satisfaction this time. "No, *doctor*, they will prove the opposite. You never expected the forgery to be discovered."

"Look, John. I'm asking—no, I'm begging you to let me see the Bonvalet. To check whether it's the same painting I authenticated. Surely you want to know as much as I do."

"Absolutely out of the question. Mr. Buchanan personally put the notes in the safe early yesterday morning when the painting was delivered, and no one is allowed access. By tomorrow, we'll have proof of your fraud, and the whole matter will be referred to the police."

From the way he was leaning forward across his desk and staring at her with eyebrows high in expectation, John obviously hoped for a full confession right there and then. But Gemma had only one thought, and it was making her ill: Mack had taken her notes from her workroom before she'd met him at the Enright. All through their so-called lovemaking yesterday, he'd kept that deceit to himself.

"However," John continued into the silence, "McCallister's may be prepared to drop the charges in exchange for a full confession and recovery of the $50 million. As you can appreciate,

McCallister's would prefer to keep this quiet, but you must cooperate fully."

She watched dumbly as he rested his elbows on the desk and pressed his fingertips together, savoring the anticipation of his next words. "You have one chance, Dr. Gilmore. Talk to me now, or go to prison."

Gemma couldn't have said a word if she tried. Not with her breath seized in her lungs to the point of dizziness. Prison. The word rang so loudly that it took her a moment to realize it wasn't in her head. The whole building was ringing. The fire alarm had gone off.

John was already at the door by the time she stumbled to her feet.

"Damn. I forgot to cancel the fire drill. You go ahead. Use the stairwell; the elevators will be out. I'll call the fire department and let them know."

Gemma made her way into the tenth-floor stairwell. She couldn't hear anyone coming down the stairs above her or any noises drifting up from below. The place was deserted, but that was to be expected if McCallister's security system was out. Nobody would be allowed to stay after five thirty.

She worked her way down the stairs, stopping at the fourth floor to take a breath. She was one floor below her workroom. She rarely went to the fourth—which held the safe.

Safe!

The numbers she'd memorized from Mack's wallet. They had to be to McCallister's safe.

She leaned against the banister and stared at the half-open fire exit - beckoning her like it was the gateway to salvation itself. Slipping her fingers into her bag, she clutched her phone and ran her thumb over the screen, her mind whirling with the significance of her discovery. She had the combination. Her notes were in that safe and, more importantly, so was the Bonvalet. She could check the work right now. She knew Bonvalet better than anyone. It would take only a few minutes to examine the painting, and then she would know if it was the same one she'd seen three weeks ago. If it were, John Allen would be groveling for forgiveness. And if it was a forgery, she could ... what?

Nothing. She couldn't do anything. Her notes wouldn't match. She'd be charged with fraud. There'd be a trial. Whether she was found guilty or innocent, it wouldn't matter. Her career would be over.

Mack Buchanan had destroyed her. He'd taken her career. He had no feelings. No conscience. She'd known all along he was dangerous. But even so, she'd still underestimated what he was capable of.

No, she wouldn't give that jerk the satisfaction of making her cry. But she would sit down to think things through.

The alarm shut off a minute later, but Gemma stayed put on the cold concrete step, staring at that half-open door.

Thinking.

There was something she'd missed.

Okay, first she'd found the safe combination in Mack's wallet, which in itself was a little strange. Why a set of numbers and nothing else? Then Lucy had called and mentioned the security system was down. That was innocent enough, as it had been down a few times lately. But then John Allen had asked her to meet him at McCallister's—at a time when he knew the building would be empty.

Now today, the fire alarm had gone off, and John had told her to take the stairs by herself, knowing she would go past the floor where the safe was. It was all too convenient. Too arranged.

Too obvious.

Talk about being slow on the uptake. It was a trap. Mack wanted her to go into the safe to check the painting and her notes. She'd be caught and arrested. Guilty as charged.

For all she knew, he was probably waiting within ten feet of her right now, ready to cuff her and drag her away.

"Go to hell, Mack Buchanan," she said out loud, enjoying the sound echoing up and down the stairwell. She said it again, shouting this time for his benefit. It felt good. Good enough to grow some backbone and deal with him once and for all. Even if she did go to prison, she'd damn well go down fighting. And what's more, she didn't care if he was listening to her right now.

She should let Kyle know what had happened, but he would only start on her case again. Pulling her phone out of her bag, she called Lucy. She needed to be warned.

A male answered with a tentative, "Hello."

"Jamie?"

He sounded shy and more than a little embarrassed. "Oh, hi Gem. Lucy's ... well, she can't come to the phone right now."

Oh. Lucy certainly hadn't wasted much time getting to know the love of her life. Still, Gemma hadn't exactly kept her own sexual urges under control. "That's okay. I need to talk to you both anyway. The thing is, Mack Buchanan knows you and Lucy were looking for my notes."

"Oh, sure, we know that. Lucy has that covered. She heard him talking to John Allen about locking your Bonvalet stuff in the safe."

So, Mack *had* planned it all. "Anything else?"

"Here's Lucy now."

"Hi, GG. What ya want to know?"

Gemma caught the extra bubble in Lucy's voice. She was happy. Excited at being with Jamie. It seemed a shame to flatten it.

"I'm sorry, Lucy, but you need to know. John Allen is threatening to refer you and Jamie to the police."

"Yeah, we know."

How did the girl do it? "You know? How?"

Lucy sounded impatient now. "That's *so* not important. The thing is, grumpy Allen was in the safe yesterday morning, right after Big Mack locked it."

Gemma's backside almost slipped off the step when she straightened in astonishment. So much for John taking any notice of Mack's order to stay out of the safe. Of course, it didn't mean he was doing anything wrong. As the operations manager and a trusted employee of McCallister's for ten years, he was entitled to go into the safe whenever he liked. It was probably about something that had nothing to do with the Bonvalet or her notes for that matter.

"Are you still there?" Lucy's voice broke into her thoughts.

"I'm here. Anything else?"

"I reckon Big Mack is a spy or something."

A James Bond with an exploding wallet "Maybe. Anyway, please be careful, Lucy."

Her concern was rewarded with a loud snort. "Of course, silly. You know, Jamie's totally excellent at—"

Lord, she so didn't need to know.

"That's great, sweetie," she interrupted quickly. "Promise me you'll be careful."

As usual, she might as well be talking to the walls for all the good it did. "You're such a worrywart, GG. Anyway, gotta go."

A second later, Lucy was gone. Pushing herself to her feet, Gemma started down the stairs again, then stopped. Dragging her phone out of her bag again, she called him.

He answered immediately, making Gemma wonder if he expected her call. Maybe he was watching her right now?

"Are you okay?"

Her anger flared. What an act.

"Like you would care. Your plan didn't work!"

She heard his small intake of breath. "Where are you?"

"Where are *you*, Mr. Buchanan?"

"I'll come and get you."

Like she'd go anywhere with him ever again. Definitely not to a hotel, for sure. A restaurant wouldn't do either. Too public. What she had to say would involve shouting. Lots of shouting. She might even throw something at him.

"We need to talk. My apartment in an hour. Be there or else."

Or else what? It sounded ridiculous threatening the Titan god of destruction—the man was twice her size and Lord knows how many times stronger.

"An hour." She thought she detected a hint of amusement in his voice.

She hung up on him.

By the time she'd made it to the ground floor and was out in the warm evening air, she felt so much better.

It was time to take charge. Kyle had warned her to stay away from Mack. Well, she would. Right after she'd told Mack what a lowlife he was.

It wouldn't be difficult. After all, he was just a man. Not a Titan.

CHAPTER NINE

Okay, so the trap wasn't a good idea.

Just routine, Mack had told himself a hundred times all the way across town to her apartment. As a suspect, Gemma had to know this could happen. But he already knew she wouldn't see it that way. Right now, he was just a bastard who'd screwed her, then set her up.

And she was right, plain and simple.

He might be relieved that she hadn't fallen for it, but there was no use in telling her that. Fact was he no longer believed she was involved in the fraud.

Well, almost.

Mack was halfway through his knock when the door flew open with a whoosh. Her expression he could only guess at—he was totally focused on everything below her neck. And Jesus, if the sight of black hot pants and a white, supershort tank top didn't test his restraint to the limit, he had yet to figure what the hell would. But dammit, he wasn't going to go there. Temptation incarnate might be standing three feet away, but it was time to finally get professional and stop thinking with his dick.

Keep a lid on things, Buchanan.

Her eyes fell suspiciously on the brown bag in his hand. "What's *that?*"

Mack looked up and forced a grin, fighting his last brain cell not to take another eyeful of everything she'd put on display for him. An invitation? Hardly. With that scowl, he'd be lucky to get out alive.

"I'm guessing you haven't eaten."

Her blue eyes flashed.

"I didn't invite you here to eat."

Apart from giving him an ear-bashing about what a bastard he was, exactly what did she want him here for? Not to kiss and make up, that was for sure. There had to be some reason, even it was just to tease him with a show of skin. She'd done that before. She was damned good at it.

"As I remember, it was more of an order." Mack held the bag out like a peace offering. "You like Italian?"

She glared at the bag, then swept a less-than-casual glance over his jeans and T-shirt before turning away, sashaying herself to the kitchen, her ass displayed to perfection in the tight shorts, her dark hair a silky tumble down her back. One thing was for sure: the heat between them hadn't cooled any.

She slapped two table mats on the counter, followed by plates, cutlery, and glasses, then stood with a hand on her hip, waiting for him to catch up, still scowling.

"Well, what did you bring?"

She might be madder than a hornet, but her interest in food constituted some progress. On his part, it gave him something to think about other than what was under that top. Nothing, from what he could tell.

"Pasta and a bottle of red." He emptied the bag and gestured for a bottle opener. While he dealt with the wine, she opened the cartons of food and arranged two stools, one on each side of the counter. She wanted distance between them, and he couldn't say he minded. Right now, he needed all the distance he could get. Hell, did she have to look so damned tempting?

Mack filled two glasses and pushed one across the counter toward her. If she weren't so mad, this could almost pass for a cozy dinner.

"Fettuccini or penne?" he asked super politely.

Mack hadn't really expected her to eat with him, but to his surprise, she leaned forward to check the contents, her top slipping sideways to reveal a bare shoulder. Yeah, nothing under there but those perky breasts just begging for his touch.

"Penne, I guess."

What? Mack dragged his mind back to the food, grateful for the distraction. He tipped the penne onto a plate while she drummed her fingers on her hip.

"Why did you do it?"

Mack knew the question would come sooner rather than later, but it still caught him unprepared. What to say? That this was just standard procedure for him and it could have been much worse? That, for a suspect, she'd gotten off lightly?

"It's what I do."

When she picked up her wine, he held his breath, half-expecting her to hurl it at him, but she took a gulp and set it down with a thump. "Is that all you can say, you—you—jerk?"

For a fact, it was, considering his line of work. "If it's any consolation, I'm glad you didn't do it."

"You liar!" She was shouting now.

Mack winced at the loathing in her voice. "I know it's difficult—"

"Were you at McCallister's? Waiting for me to go into the safe?" He watched her small hands ball into fists on the countertop, seriously wondering if she was about to put them to use on him.

He slid onto a stool and loaded his plate with fettuccine, aware that her eyes were following his every move. "No, I was at my apartment," he answered quietly.

"And where's that?" she snapped.

He tried for calm again. "How about we eat first, then talk."

She plunked herself down on her stool, ignoring the food, her eyes still glued to his face. "How about you tell me who you work for?"

Mack nodded toward her plate. "It's good. Try some."

She started pushing her food around with her fork, frowning—whether in anger or thought he couldn't tell, but it was probably both.

"Lucy thinks you're a spy. Are you?"

Lucy Barton. A smart little thing, with a keen nose for sniffing out information. The girl was pretty damn good at it, too. He chuckled inwardly at the memory.

"I thought *she* was the spy. Her and that friend of hers, Jamie O'Mara."

Her brow shot up in alarm. "They were only trying to help. You won't have them fired, will you?"

"Not if they stay out of it."

He made his voice serious, although to be honest, they hadn't been a problem. Nosy, yes, but nothing compared to what he was used to. In fact, he'd quite enjoyed having a pair of amateur sleuths on his tail.

"Stay out of *what*? Isn't it about time you told me what you do?"

"Not possible," he answered evenly. She was persistent; he had to give her that. A quality he normally admired, but right now he wished she didn't have so damned much of it.

His answer set her off again.

"Why not? Isn't it the least you can do after everything that happened?"

She was furious. And desperately hurt. Mack set his fork down and briefly closed his eyes. He'd put her through hell. Maybe he should give her a few details. No, on second thought, that would only lead to more questions he couldn't answer without breaching security. Fuck, he must be going soft in the head to even consider it. But then, he'd barely had a rational thought since first laying eyes on her. And dammit, it wasn't just her body that was wreaking hell with his judgment.

Yesterday at the hotel had given him a glimpse of what he might have had if he hadn't pursued a career in intelligence. A woman to love. Being loved. He'd wanted to serve his country in the most elite military undercover unit, but it had come at a cost. Spending months in dangerous situations had hardened him to the point where he could no longer afford to care. At thirty-two, he was already a veteran in his field and considered one of the best. Yet he couldn't deny he liked his work, thrived on the danger and the not knowing where he'd be sent next. All he knew was that wherever it was, he'd be helping to protect the lives of innocent people.

And then all this had happened. A simple, no-action, no-stress art fraud job—time off, a semi vacation to give his body time to recover. Never had he expected the work to come with a complication in the form of Gemma Gilmore. If she were any other woman, he'd enjoy her and then walk away when he needed to. It had always been that easy, even necessary in a job where there was no guarantee of survival.

But this woman, with her unforgettable eyes that could snare him in a heartbeat, he couldn't walk away from. He'd invested more of himself emotionally in her than in any woman—and he barely knew her. She was gutsy, but had a softness and vulnerability that constantly tested his urge to protect her. His job was to get to the truth, but sitting here right now, looking into those beautiful eyes sparking with anger and hurt, he didn't much like his job.

He opened his mouth, ready to explain why he couldn't tell her, when she barked another question. "How did you get that wound on your side? Pity it didn't find your heart."

Mack gave up on his plan and went back to eating.

"Well, who stabbed you?"

"You wouldn't know him. Eat." He pointed his fork at her plate.

Her glare might be able to destroy his retinas at fifty feet, but at least she'd decided to try the penne, even if it was just to pick at the olives. He did his best not to notice when her top slipped further down as she reached for her glass. It was all he could do not to hurdle the counter and rip the thing clear off her body. Man, she sorely tested him.

As if sensing his predatory thought, she straightened and waited until he looked up and met her gaze, her eyes mocking.

"Something wrong, Mr. Buchanan?"

"Why did you go into my wallet?" he said between his teeth, steering the conversation to something—anything—to quell the thought of relieving her of that top.

She didn't answer, so he pushed harder.

"It was a stupid thing to do. A big risk to take. Why?"

Still no answer. Mack was about to ask again when she looked up, two faint vertical lines appearing between her dark brows while she thought.

"I ... I just thought the numbers must mean something. Actually ... " She paused to bite her lip. "It was Kyle who figured out it was a safe combination."

So, he was right. She'd gone straight from the hotel to see Lawrence. Christ, this was just what he needed: jealous of that stuffed shirt. Mack swallowed the lump of resentment rising up his throat. "So what did he advise you to do?"

"That's none of your business."

"Fair enough. So why did you break off your engagement?" he asked on an impulse, telling himself he had good reason to know, although it was nothing more than his damned curiosity getting the better of him. Frankly, he couldn't imagine those two together. The fit didn't seem right, but then, when it came down to it, he knew almost nothing about her, apart from the fact that she was a fiery little thing.

Her chin angled defiantly. "That's none of your business, either."

"In other words, he screwed the office junior?"

No fucking way. There was no mistaking that horrified expression. Old Straight-Laced had cheated on her. Man, that was the last thing he expected, considering Kyle had the incredibly sensual Gemma waiting for him at home. That, and the fact the guy just didn't seem the type to stray.

"Sorry, I didn't mean to … "

He paused, waiting for a response, but she'd gone silent, so he went on, now wishing he'd kept his frigging mouth shut.

"That must've been tough." Obviously, he'd hit a sore point. Maybe she still wanted her ex. "More wine?"

He'd had only just lifted the bottle when she spoke softly.

"It was … Kyle was weak. I guess, under the circumstances, it was understandable. After all, I did neglect him."

Jesus, did she actually blame herself? Why did women do that?

He lowered the bottle. "How so?"

She started twirling her glass around and around on the countertop as if it might offer up an explanation. "I was doing my doctorate. Between McCallister's and writing my dissertation, I never had any time for anything else. But it was only to be for a few months and then—well, by that time Miranda had started at Cooper and Forney's, and"—she stopped to moisten her lips—"after that it was over. The big scene. The ring returned. My mother blaming me for pushing Kyle into Miranda's arms."

"You want him back?" he asked quietly. He so shouldn't do this, but dammit, he had to know.

"No."

He caught the frustration in her tone. She must have been asked that question a hundred times. Mack was more curious now.

"Yet you went to Venice with him."

She drained her glass in one gulp before setting it down to renew the twirling.

"It was Kyle's idea. He thought we could work things out, make a fresh start." She gave a short, forced burst of laughter. "At least I got to see Venetian art."

Bitterness peppered her response. Whatever their relationship had been, he could only guess. Even so, he couldn't picture them in a hotel room, fucking their brains out for hours on end.

She stared him straight in the eyes. "We *were* happy at one time." It was as if she'd read his thoughts.

He grimaced, suddenly not wanting to know any more about her and her ex. Okay, so he wasn't the most sensitive guy when it came to women and their myriad problems. But dammit, he wasn't up for a Dr. Phil session over that jackass. He got to his feet.

"Right, how about I make coffee?"

Mack had barely taken two steps when the question came.

"Do you still think I'm guilty?"

He sat down again and considered for a moment. Gemma couldn't be guilty. And if that was his idiot libido getting the better of him again, then so be it.

"No."

She blinked in surprise. "Oh. So what changed your mind?"

"For a start, you'd be on a flight to somewhere safe by now, instead of hammering me with questions." He nudged her plate with a finger, trying to sound serious. "Now be a good girl and finish your penne."

She puckered her lips in a pout, sending him a sulky look from under her lashes. Cute.

"I don't like being told what to do."

Mack didn't miss the snag of arousal in her voice. True, he'd been listening for it. He grinned. Yep, this was better.

"Yeah, you do."

Two spots of red flared high on her cheeks. Plenty of attitude, but his words had heated her. Not that he was having a cool moment himself. Just a hint of her sexual need had sent most of his blood south. At this rate, they'd be replaying yesterday's sex marathon right here on her kitchen countertop.

"Would you like me to come over there and prove it?" he asked quietly.

"You really think I'd want you *now*?" Her eyes widened in disbelief.

Going by the way she was checking out his chest, she did.

"Uh-huh, that's exactly what I think." Sexual awareness ping-ponged between them.

"God, you're so full of yourself."

He grinned, really enjoying himself now. "Well, you did say I was—who was it? Oh yeah, Perses."

She slid him a sly look. "A Titan who destroys things, that's you. Kyle says you're dangerous."

Fair comment. He'd been told that more than once.

"What else did he say?"

"That I should stay away from you."

He leaned forward to snare her gaze in his, seeing the wariness creep into the blue depths.

"In that case, Dr. Gilmore, why *did* you order me here?"

Her chin went up. "Not for what you think."

Even snooty, she was one big turn-on.

"And what *am* I thinking?"

She shrugged, not quite avoiding his gaze. "How would I know?"

He dropped his voice. "Come here, and I'll tell you."

"No way!"

Yeah, still touchy, but that was mostly for show. From the way her full lips had parted and her blue eyes deepened to navy pools, she wanted him.

But Mack held back. She expected him to go get her—to pick her up and carry her into her bedroom and take her. But as tempting as the thought was, he wanted her to come to him.

Not that he fully understood his own reasoning, but right now, it mattered that this captivating woman make the first move.

She looked puzzled, unsure of what to do with the situation. Mack waited, wondering how long it would take for the penny to drop—maybe it wouldn't drop, and he'd have to go get her after all. But just when he decided to have her right there in her kitchen, she slowly slid off her stool and walked around the counter to stand in front of him.

She stared at him solemnly.

"Tell me."

"What, sweetheart?" Mack frowned, confused.

She didn't answer him. Instead, she put a hand on each of his shoulders and pulled herself onto his lap to straddle him, her eyes laced with mischief.

"Tell me what you're thinking."

He tangled his fingers in her hair, angled her head to kiss her, held her hard to his mouth, plunged his tongue deep. That they were here, doing this, didn't really surprise him. Before even setting foot in her apartment, he'd half-known this would happen. From the get-go, they'd operated on sexual chemistry. Instant. Spontaneous. There was no fighting it. It was as real as the beautiful mouth that he was kissing. She felt so right in his arms. Everything about her was right, and that was the trouble. He flat-out couldn't resist her.

She was kissing along his jaw now, the tip of her tongue scraping across his beard bristles.

"Tell me, Perses," she whispered, dipping down to bite his neck like she meant business. "Tell me now, or else." She nipped him hard on his tattoo.

Feisty, and so damned sexy.

"It's best I show you."

In one swift movement, he whipped her top over her head, tossing it on the floor. If he saw Gemma like this a million times, he'd never stop marveling at her beauty and the stark contrast of her pale slenderness to his own sun-darkened body with its scarred flesh.

Gently, Mack cupped her curvy little breasts, savoring their snug fit in his palms. Her nipples were incredibly sensitive—just the lightest brush of his thumbs was enough to elicit a small moan. He bent her back over his arm to close his mouth over a rosy peak, swirled his tongue around the areola, growling with pleasure when she rose to his mouth.

She whimpered when he explored the other breast; her fingers dug into his shoulders as he dragged his mouth ultraslow from the nub, repeating the process over and over. When she started squirming against the bulge in his jeans, he almost lost it.

Definitely time to get things moving.

He glanced around the lounge. The sofa looked more or less okay for the job—not great, but roomier than her bed.

His hands were half-under her butt, ready to lift her, when she wriggled herself back and started undoing his jeans, giving a small exhalation of frustration as she struggled with the last two buttons. Not surprising, considering the amount of tension he had on them.

Finally, she wrenched them undone and, sighing in triumph, freed his cock. His pulse shot to heart-attack levels when she ran a thumb over the head, spreading a drop of liquid around the ridge—all the while licking at her bottom lip like she'd just been given a fat lollipop to play with. It seemed so natural to her Mack doubted she even realized she was doing it.

He knew what she had in mind, but that would have to wait. Jesus Christ, he needed her out of those shorts. Fast. Slipping his hands back under her butt, he carried her to the sofa and sat her down, dragging off her shorts and black panties. Pushing her legs wide, he fell to his knees to stroke along her with the tip of his tongue, dipping an exploratory finger into her body.

Her moan was so loud he looked up, startled. Had he'd done something wrong? Hard to tell with her head thrown back and her hands gripping the sofa cushions like that. But then she wriggled forward, trying to connect herself to his mouth, so he slipped a second finger into her wetness and kissed along the inside of her thighs.

She rocked up, urging him for more contact, so he licked along her bare folds and up over the landing strip. Her hips pumped in response. He did it again. And again.

"You taste incredible, babe."

Man, he should stretch this out, enjoy her little moans and gasps before letting her come. But from the way her thighs were trembling, he doubted she'd last much longer anyway.

His tongue had barely touched her clit when he felt the telltale tightening around his fingers. She was so close that he'd never hold her back. Curling an arm around her butt to lift her hips, he held her flush to his mouth, concentrating on that single hot spot that would send her over the edge. By now she was writhing so hard he had to tighten his hold to keep her steady.

"Oh, God ... Mack ... *Mack*!"

He snarled pure primal satisfaction at the sound. He increased the pressure, drawing more of her into his mouth. He was going to make her come so hard she'd never forget it. Seconds later, she climaxed—crying out, sobbing, spreading wide as he tongued her over the brink.

He looked up, wiped his mouth, and grinned.

"Fuck, you are one sexy woman, Dr. Gilmore."

She peered seductively down her body at him, arching and stretching like a contented cat.

"Thank you, Perses."

He laughed and eased his fingers out of her body. She was so tight from her orgasm that he wondered, and not for the first time, if he'd fit when he took her. But hell, he was going to find out. Right now.

He'd only just pushed off his jeans and briefs when she was on her knees.

"Oh, Jesus," he groaned when her soft mouth closed over the head of his dick.

Mack stood absolutely still, transfixed by the sight of Gemma's head bobbing over him, her long hair spread like a velvet cloud around her pale shoulders. She was making little humming noises that he could actually feel vibrating down his length, amplifying the pleasure with each draw of her mouth.

She was amazing, and if he didn't sit down, he'd fall down.

He didn't try to speak—he doubted he could utter a word anyway. He just turned and dropped like a lump of concrete onto the sofa. It took her all of three seconds to find him again.

If his life had depended on it, he couldn't have torn his eyes away from the sight of Gemma's soft mouth sliding up and down on him, pausing every so often to lick along the underside of his cock before taking him in again.

"So beautiful," she murmured, as more of him disappeared into her mouth. Mack clenched his jaw against the raw pleasure building at the base of his cock. He pushed her hair back to watch her—the incredible slide of her lips, her dark lashes resting on her cheeks as she drew on him again and again.

He felt her gag. He grabbed a fistful of her hair and tried to pull her back, but she wouldn't budge, and he was too drugged with pleasure to make any real effort to stop her. She was sucking him harder now, concentrating on making him come. He couldn't hang on. It was too much. Too good. He tensed as he realized what was about to happen. "Sweetheart, I can't—" he warned, wanting to give her the option to pull back. But she took no notice, working her mouth and fingers in an intoxicating, glorious rhythm that, moments later, had milked every last drop from him.

So much for keeping a lid on things.

CHAPTER TEN

Gemma woke to the smell of coffee, aftershave, and man.

It felt so totally delicious with her face buried in the pillow where Mack's head had been. She was worn out, but in the most perfect way. Seriously though, it wasn't right. She shouldn't feel delicious. She should feel guilty.

Gemma rolled over and stared at the ceiling. Déjà vu, that's what she'd done. Yes, she'd been weak and silly for letting him stay, and, yes, she would never learn her lesson when it came to this gorgeous man.

Plus he'd hogged the bed.

And what was he doing in her kitchen? Going by the sounds of crockery and cutlery being moved around, he had to be fixing something other than coffee. Somehow, she couldn't imagine the man of mystery doing anything domestic.

But apart from that, the burning question was, did he really no longer think she was involved in the fraud? Maybe he'd decided to give her the benefit of the doubt. Then again, it could just be another one of his traps. In any event, she would call John Allen this morning and tell him that Mack Buchanan knew she was innocent. McCallister's would have no choice but to give her back her job.

But hell, what was he doing now? He must have found her new cast-iron skillet set to play with. Grabbing his scrunched-up T-shirt from the floor, Gemma pulled it over her head and checked for fit. It finished halfway down her thighs, but the funny thing was she'd never felt sexier.

Two steps and she was in the kitchen. Oh Lord, now there was a sight for sore eyes. Mack stood with his back to her in nothing but his jeans set low on his hips. The man had muscles she didn't even know existed. And that butt. She could stare at that 'til Christmas.

"Hi there. Did I wake you?" he asked over his shoulder.

She was so busy staring at his ass that it took her a moment to register the question. "What? Oh, no. Can I do anything?"

"Not necessary. Eggs okay?"

"Mmm, yes please. How did you sleep?" She already knew the answer. The poor guy had been crammed against the wall for most of the night. Well, except when he was on top of her or she was on top of him.

He turned, a soft smile spreading across his face like a warm treat. "Let's just say your grandmother has a lot to answer for."

She laughed. "I'll tell her that when I see her."

"Right." His eyes drifted down her body. "You look good in that."

Even the smallest compliment from him could heat her body.

"In that case, I'm keeping it."

His brow went up. "Yeah?"

"Uh-huh."

He turned back to the pan, so Gemma snuggled her face between his shoulder blades, filling her lungs with his warm scent. His deep voice rumbled into her cheek as he moved away to take plates from the dish rack. "It's ready. Have a seat."

She sighed at the loss, pulling herself onto a stool to watch him pile scrambled eggs onto plates and set them on the counter, followed by toast and steaming mugs of coffee. Like this, all mellowed-out, he was kind of adorable.

Her mouth was watering by the time he'd found knives and forks. A night of lovemaking with a Titan could work up a powerful appetite. As if he had read her mind, he grinned. "I thought you'd be hungry." He slid onto a stool beside her, still smiling in that quiet, self-assured, totally delicious way.

"Maybe, just a little." She tucked into the eggs and a minute later realized she'd bolted most of her breakfast before he'd even started on his. Instead, he was watching her. Still smiling.

She set her fork down and sipped at her coffee, waiting for him to catch up.

"So where did you learn to cook?" she asked casually. Querying him about anything, even cooking, was risky, considering how poorly he took to questions. But surely, after spending a night together, it was safe to ask.

To her surprise, he winked at her.

"Just something I picked up."

They ate in silence for a while, giving Gemma time to work up courage for her next question. She was going to do this—needed to do this. Last night was a write-off. He'd told her zilch. But this morning was a different story. He believed her. Surely, that was enough for her to be able to trust him and vice versa.

Here goes nothing, Gemma.

"You never give anything away, do you?" She waited, and when nothing came, she blurted out, "Where were you born?"

"Chicago," he answered without hesitation, still eating.

Oh, wow. This was good. "And where did you go to school?" she asked, trying to keep her tone casual, despite her rising excitement about finally getting some answers.

He flicked a glance in her direction before turning back to his plate. It was so fast she couldn't tell whether it was friendly or one of his "don't ask me" looks.

"Columbia ... " he paused, "for a while."

Okay, that was more cautious.

"Then where?"

"Out of state."

This wasn't so good, especially now that his dark brow was drawn low in warning. She plunged on, determined to get something useful out of him.

"And how did you get into ... the work you do?"

He set his fork down, his hazel eyes steady on hers. "Let's just say I wanted to be a public servant."

"So you work for the government?"

No answer. Gemma remembered what Kyle had said. "Military intelligence? That's it, isn't it?"

Still no answer. Just another warning look to let her know not to push it. Despite everything they'd done last night—hell, practically every day since this whole thing had started—he could still switch on that hard edge in a millisecond. And dammit if it wasn't that dangerous, unknown part of him that that made him so compelling. Apparently, she had some unconscious thing for bad boys. *Something else to tell the therapist.*

She sighed, "I know. You can't tell me."

"So how long have you had this place?" he asked, topping up her coffee.

It would serve him right if she told him to mind his own business.

"Three years. I invested every penny I had to make the deposit. The place is too small, really, but the view of the park is worth it."

He looked around. "It's nice. Suits you."

"Thanks. What's your home like ... ?" Gemma trailed off. Of course, he wouldn't tell her. It seemed they had nothing to talk about, other than art fraud and sex.

To her surprise, he grinned and leaned over to ruffle her hair like she was some inquisitive kid asking what made the sky blue.

"Actually, I have a beach house in Maine. We used to go there a lot." He paused for a moment, as if recalling something. "But it's been a while."

She had trouble absorbing his statement. Out of the blue, he'd told her something about his life. But the real surprise was that he'd said *we*. That could mean anything: his parents, his siblings. His *wife*. She forced the thought away and got up to put her plate and cutlery in the sink, suddenly not wanting to know and, at the same time, angry at herself for caring.

"I've only been to Bar Harbor, and that was just for a weekend. More coffee?"

"No, I'm good." He came to stand behind her, slipping his arms around her waist, bending to rest his chin on the top of her head. She leaned her head back against his chest and closed her eyes, savoring the sensation of being enclosed in his arms.

"I know you're curious about what I do, Gemma, but it's not something I can talk about. Can you understand that?"

No, frankly, she couldn't. Not after her life had turned belly up—and he was smack in the middle of whatever was going on. Okay, so he didn't tolerate questions, but dammit, why should she just give up?

"But I'm not a suspect anymore, Mack. Why *can't* you talk about it? At least tell me why you can't tell me."

"I can't tell you that."

"You're really annoying, you know that?"

He laughed and kissed her hair. "Noted. Look, all I can tell you is that I don't want to see you hurt." His big hand enclosed hers. "I care about what happens to you. A lot."

Gemma warmed to the words, gaining confidence. "Then *why* … ?"

He turned her around to face him, his eyes soft on hers, but she knew it was a deliberate distraction. He'd shut down.

"Do you have any idea what you do to me, sweetheart?"

"Irritate the hell out of you with questions," she answered glibly, trying to ignore his chest in front of her. So perfect, with its sprinkling of dark hair spread over an acre of tanned muscle.

"Yeah, well, apart from that." A laugh rumbled above her head.

"I think I know," she whispered, unable to quell a shiver of need as his hand pressed to the small of her back. She shouldn't lose her head this time. She really shouldn't. Kyle was right: She needed to show some sense.

"Well, just to be sure you know." He cleared a space between the breakfast dishes and, lifting her, sat her on the countertop. He settled his hips between her legs, and Gemma lost her last thought of being sensible. Mack Buchanan. The strong, infuriatingly stubborn man she couldn't get enough of.

He traced his thumb along her bottom lip. "For a start, you make me want to kiss you."

She desperately wanted that, too.

His lips found hers, and she moaned until he laughed softly against her mouth. Lifting his head, he was still smiling.

"Then you make me want to kiss you, right here."

Beard bristles scraped along her skin as he nosed her hair aside to kiss at a spot below her ear. She angled her head, inviting him to kiss more of her, loving the rough feel of him on her neck. He paused. She waited, trembling with anticipation.

"Then there's this." A hand was under the tee now, sliding up to her breast, his fingers gently plucking at her nipple. "And this." His other hand slipped up the inside of her thigh to trace a slow path along her sex, pausing to press her clit.

"And this ... "

She wriggled forward. "But you're forgetting something," she murmured, undoing his jeans, working her hand inside to find him. She sighed in satisfaction when he shuddered under her slow caress.

He wasn't taking his time now. Before she'd even started to have her own fun, he dragged a condom from his jeans and freed it from the wrapper before pushing her hand away. She licked at her lip, watching him roll the rubber down the thick shaft.

He laughed softly, making her look up. "What?" she asked, confused.

"Oh nothing. Just that tongue of yours."

"What about my tongue?"

He leaned forward to nip at her bottom lip with his teeth before kissing her long and hard, and Gemma forgot about her tongue, other than to put it in his mouth.

He pulled her forward until her butt was hanging half-off the counter, her legs dangling on either side of his hips.

"Now this…"

She watched him ease himself into her body. Slowly, almost lazily, he pushed forward until she was filled up with him, loving the sensation of only just being able to take him.

"And this…"

She stared, fascinated, at where he ended and she began. Dear God, it was like some pornographic close-up. Both of them watched his shaft emerging from her body, glistening with her wetness before disappearing into her again.

For Gemma, it was beyond erotic. It was mesmerizing. She edged her knees wider, offering more of herself. He growled in appreciation, pulled out of her completely to rub his cock over her clit, then pushed into her again in one long, satisfying plunge. She flashed a look up to his face, then looked down, not wanting to miss a thing.

"And this…"

His voice was rough as he pulled his hand away to close the small gap between them. She braced herself. He'd primed her carefully, and she was more than ready for everything he was about to give her.

With one hand braced on the countertop for support, he slid his other arm around her waist to hold her steady to his hips before pushing into her. Hard and purposeful now. A glorious succession of deep, orgasm-seeking strokes that repeatedly drove her back against his arm. He filled her body and her senses. Her world was him. His rhythm. His strength. His passion.

His mouth snagged her hair. "Okay, babe?"

Gemma hummed into the dip of his shoulder. Her hands slipped around his chest as far as she could reach, trying to hang on through his powerful drives. It didn't matter. He had her fastened in his hold, leaving her with nothing to do but concentrate on the luscious sensation building between her legs.

She trembled as the familiar tightening in her core began its steady spiral toward resolution. She arched back, clutching at his biceps, feeling them tense under her fingers as he pulled her forward again, leaving nothing between them but the heat of their union. She couldn't stop her cry of pleasure.

She was too weak to move, but he wasn't finished with her. He hadn't come. She felt herself lifted almost clear of the countertop, felt him adjust his stance against her, then thrust into her. Long, powerful strokes that, incredibly, made her body throb for release again. Friction almost too blissful to bear.

"Come for me."

His clenched-jaw command was all it took. Her eyes flickered shut as sweet spasms enveloped her again. She felt him shudder against her, and Gemma opened her eyes to see his face locked in his grimace of lust. Oh, how she loved that she could do that to him. To have that power over this sexy, exciting man.

His fingers dug into her waist as he surged into her body. He was coming. "Gemma ... Gemma," he groaned, and the sound sang sweet in her ears.

"Mack," she whispered after he had finally eased his hold on her and her breathing had settled enough to speak.

"Yeah?"

"How ... what's going to happen?" She wanted to add "with us" but couldn't pluck up the courage to ask something so personal.

He settled his chin on the top of her head. "We wait and see."

What did that mean? She decided on a safer topic.

"Mack."

"I'm still here."

Cheeky devil.

"You need a shave."

He grunted. "Right. Do you have anything?"

"Only a lady-shave thingy. I wax."

He looked down. "I can see that. And very nice it is, too." He swiped his beard across her cheek, making her squeal. "Mind if I use your shower?"

She pinched his butt in retaliation.

"Only if I can wash your back."

"Sounds good."

He slipped out of her, and Gemma sat on the counter watching him remove the condom and head for the bathroom. The man was totally delicious, in a lethal kind of way. An enigma wrapped in a mystery—that was Mack. But at least she now knew where he was raised, where he went to college, and that he had a house in Maine.

The shower was running, and she was halfway to the bathroom to join him, when her doorbell buzzed.

Damn. Not now. Whoever it was, they could just go away. The door buzzed again as she reached the bathroom door. She stood on the spot, dithering. It was most likely Beth from upstairs, wanting to go out for Sunday breakfast or shopping or maybe take in a movie. But then, Beth usually called first.

She ambled resentfully to the door, rehearsing her "this isn't a good time" spiel. Beth wouldn't mind being turned away. If anything, her sex-mad neighbor would hoot with glee that Gemma had finally ended her man-drought.

"I need to talk to you."

Oh, dear God. Kyle.

She took a horrified step back, stupidly giving him enough space to stride past her into the apartment. "It's looking bad, Gem. Really bad. We need to think this through. The main thing is it's just his word against yours. As long as we don't panic, this can be dealt with quickly. At least we have a few minutes."

"Why are you … ?" She put a hand to her head, trying to process Kyle's words. He was ranting. "This really isn't a good time."

Kyle shook his head in irritation. "You don't understand. The police—" He paused to look down at the oversized tee swimming on her body. Gemma could have put voice to every thought in Kyle's head.

"Jesus, what the hell?"

"Actually, I have someone here … " She paused when his eyes darted around the apartment. "I'm sorry, but you need to leave."

His voice went shrill in astonishment. "Leave? Are you mad?" He shook his head again. "We can talk about this later. Right now, get rid of him. Or if you're too embarrassed to deal with your one-night stand, I can do it."

She opened her mouth to speak, but she couldn't make any words come out.

He angled his head in the direction of her bedroom. "I take it he's in there."

"No, don't," she managed to splutter as Kyle started toward her bedroom. "He's not in there … "

Her stupid admission stopped Kyle in his tracks. He turned to look at her like she'd completely lost her mind, then snapped his head around to the bathroom. "*You!*"

Mack stood in the doorway, his jeans half-buttoned, his bare torso glistening with water. He must have only just gotten into the shower when Kyle's voice pulled him out again.

"What the hell do you want, Lawrence?"

Mack's tone would make most men think carefully before answering, but Kyle didn't seem to notice. He'd turned beet red, and Gemma watched his hands curling into fists. Oh God, Kyle was about to do something stupid.

"Get out of my fiancée's apartment, you *bastard*."

She couldn't believe the scene unfolding in front of her. Her supercontrolled ex-fiancé screaming in rage. Desperately, she tugged at the sleeve of his suit.

"Please don't, Kyle. Just go."

Kyle shook her off and strode toward the man standing calmly in the doorway. Toward the man so much bigger, stronger, and trained in God knows what.

"Buchanan, you are some piece of work," Kyle snarled, his face now inches from Mack's. "You and your so-called investigation. It was just an excuse. You just wanted to get her to some hotel for your own goddamned pleasure, you *prick*."

The insult had no visible effect on Mack. He didn't move. Not until Kyle's fist came up—and then he dodged the swing so easily it seemed like a blur. She watched in horror as Mack took a step forward, spun Kyle around, and brought his right arm up in a hold. "Take it easy, you idiot. If you try that again, I won't be so accommodating. Got it?"

Kyle seemed to visibly deflate. He nodded dumbly, and Mack let him go, shoving him forward so that he stumbled a step.

Kyle turned to her, his face raw with humiliation and anger.

"Just tell me why. I warned you he was dangerous. To stay away from him for your own sake."

"I don't have to explain anything to you. What I do—who I'm with—is none of your business anymore."

"You have no idea, do you?"

"What are you talking about?" Mack's voice growled from behind her.

It was then Kyle let out a hollow laugh. Gemma saw his expression twist in bitterness, then something else that took her a moment to decipher.

Triumph?

"I came here to warn you, Gem. As your attorney. You're to be formally questioned in connection with the Bonvalet fraud." He jabbed a finger towards Mack. "And your ... *lover* knew about this last night when you were fucking him."

Her throat constricted so tightly it seemed impossible that she would ever be able to draw a full breath again. Kyle was just making this up out of spite and jealousy. Wasn't he? She shook her head so hard her head swam.

"I don't believe you, Kyle. Besides, Mack knows I wasn't involved." She spun to face Mack. "You told me last night. Tell Kyle you believe I had nothing to do with this.

Why was he staring at her like she was a stranger?

"Mack, you do believe me, don't you?"

He stared into her terrified gaze. He seemed genuinely shocked. "Gemma, apparently the case is now with the police. I didn't know that."

Gemma met his eyes with the full force of her hurt. "But you would have known. There's no way you wouldn't have known."

"As I said, this is a police matter now."

"How could you do it, Mack? First the safe. Now this."

"Safe? What are you talking about?" Kyle broke in sharply.

"It's nothing, Kyle. Forget it." She waved him off. "So what happens now?" she asked Kyle dully.

Kyle's eyes flicked nervously to Mack as if he expected to be manhandled out of the place.

"Right. Well, the police wanted to bring you in early this morning," he answered, now in attorney mode. "But I assured them that we'd be at the station within the hour."

Her strength drained away, Gemma stumbled back and dropped to the sofa, overcome with the reality of what was about to happen to her. "But why now? You said it yourself: McCallister's doesn't have any proof.

"Well, now they have their proof."

"What are you saying?" Gemma heard her words from a long way off.

"They've located the forger."

She blinked, not understanding. "But that's good—isn't it?"

"Hardly. He's named you as his accomplice."

CHAPTER ELEVEN

"She doesn't look the type, does she?"

"I guess not," Mack agreed, turning to take another look through the one-way mirror at Gemma sitting in the interview room. She looked genuinely terrified. There was no faking the trembling hands or ghost-white face. This had to be a first for her.

One carefully planned job that hadn't played out as expected.

"She's like some dainty Snow White. It's hard to believe that someone so young and such a bloody genius in her field would risk it all. How did she come across to you, Mack?"

He glanced over to Superintendent Ed Hutchinson, who stood with his feet braced wide, his wispy gray hair vertical from habitual raking by nicotine-stained fingers. The man was every bit the veteran cop—right down to the worn shoe leather. They'd met two years ago, when Mack's superior had consulted London Interpol over an investigation. Mack and Hutch hadn't exactly formed a friendship, but they'd shared a few beers, and Hutch had talked at length about his career in catching criminals. Mack, as usual, had revealed little about himself.

When Hutch heard of Mack's forced leave, he'd asked him to take on the art fraud job as a favor. Interpol wanted the investigation conducted outside official channels, and Mack's background made him perfect for the work. At first, he'd declined, but faced with the prospect of doing nothing for weeks while his wound healed, he'd called Hutch and accepted.

He shifted on his feet, suddenly tired. His neck felt tight, and his back muscles still ached from being unable to stretch out in Gemma's bed last night.

"Actually, she came across as genuinely shocked by the accusation."

Hutch nodded, folding thick arms over a beer paunch. "She didn't expect to get caught. Well at least we've got her."

"Yeah," Mack muttered. He brought his arm up to rest an elbow against the one-way mirror, watching Gemma lift a glass of water in shaking hands. It reminded him of that first time in her apartment. She'd been so scared of him.

"Fact is, Hutch, I believed her in the end. I could've sworn it wasn't her."

"Well, she's the kind who would make a man want to believe. Hell, even an old cynic like me would've believed her. I take it there's something personal going on? I tried to call you last night, but your phone was off." When Mack didn't answer, he chuckled. "I grant you, she'd be worth breaking a few rules over."

The sound of Kyle Lawrence's voice drew their attention to the doorway behind them.

"This is outrageous. There is absolutely no justifiable reason to hold Dr. Gilmore. I demand you release her immediately."

It was almost funny to see the jackass stride past them into the interview room and slam the door in the face of the police detective hard on his heels. The officer blew a pained sigh and looked across to Hutch.

"You want to do the interview? She's well and truly lawyered up. You'll be lucky to get her middle name, let alone anything else, with Lawrence running the show."

Hutch turned his bulk toward Mack, grinning.

"You wanna take him on?"

"Under the circumstances, maybe not." He couldn't interview Gemma with any impartiality. Barely ninety minutes ago, he'd been inside her body. He closed his eyes, letting his mind flicker through the memory of her round ass cradled in his hold when he'd sunk himself to the hilt.

By God, he'd completely lost it with this woman. How, with all his training, could he have missed all the signs of her guilt?

He could usually read body language like a book, but all the way through this investigation, there'd been nothing. Not a facial expression, a gesture, or a word. The evidence was damming. The forger had set out dates, times, and places where he and Gemma had met in Venice. The name of the hotel. It all matched. But he still found it hard to believe that she'd duped him. She could still be innocent, but realistically, he could no longer afford to believe her.

He'd been as shocked as Gemma when Kyle had broken the news about her impending arrest. She'd gone into her bedroom to dress, while Mack had waited quietly and Lawrence had paced. Emerging five minutes later in jeans and a shirt, she'd dragged on her sneakers and left with Kyle. Mack had followed a few minutes later after retrieving his T-shirt from the bed. The faint scent of her body spray still in the fabric came as a constant reminder of what they'd shared.

"You'd better do it, Hutch." He gave a dry laugh. "The idiot took a swing at me this morning, so there's no point in riling the guy more."

"You should've laid him out cold," Hutch snorted. "Would've saved us a lot of trouble. Okay, detective, let's do this."

At the sound of the interview room door being opened, Gemma looked up, her eyes flashing expectation, followed by something that Mack took to be disappointment. He switched on the intercom.

Hutch had barely dropped into his seat when he fired the first question.

"Tell us when you first met with the forger, Dr. Gilmore."

"My client doesn't have to answer that, Mister ... ?"

"Superintendent Hutchinson. British Interpol. It will be better for you, Dr. Gilmore, if you tell us everything. Now, please answer the question."

"I don't—" Kyle put a hand on Gemma's arm in warning.

"Dr. Gilmore won't respond to that. In fact, she won't answer any of your questions. My client knows nothing about this so-called art fraud."

"The forger currently goes by the name of Sorensen," Hutch continued smoothly, "although we now know he's had several aliases since he left the United States four years ago. A talented painter, by all accounts. We raided his apartment in Venice around one thirty this morning. It didn't take much for him to confess to painting the Bonvalet. Not with all the evidence found lying about. He also admitted to Dr. Gilmore's involvement."

Damn. That would have been only a few minutes after Mack had set his phone to "do not disturb," when he and Gemma had finally worn themselves out and slept. This morning, he hadn't bothered to check for messages. Just another one of his stupid mistakes.

Gemma's hands were on the table in fists. "I've never—"

"That's enough, Gem," Kyle interrupted. "Superintendent, just because this Sorensen has named Dr. Gilmore doesn't mean you have proof. He'd name anyone in exchange for a plea bargain." Kyle got to his feet. "We're leaving."

Hutch shrugged. "You're welcome to leave, Mr. Lawrence, if that's what you wish. Your client stays here."

Kyle sat down again.

"According to McCallister's, Dr. Gilmore, you went on leave for a week. To Venice."

She nodded.

"Why Venice?"

"Because Kyle ... " She stopped.

Hutch eased slowly to his feet and casually moved to stand close behind her. A deliberate move. Mack knew from experience that it sometimes worked to the point where a suspect would unwittingly give something away out of sheer nerves. She shifted in her chair, her face turned as if trying to pinpoint where he was.

Hutch leaned down to speak inches above her head. "Go on. You went to Venice with Mr. Lawrence. To the city where the forger lived? That's pretty incriminating, don't you think?"

She gave a small shake of her head.

Kyle twisted around to face Hutch. "My client won't answer any questions about Venice. Actually, it was my idea to go there on holiday, and I can personally vouch that Dr. Gilmore never met any forger. Or anyone else, for that matter."

"But you can't say for sure, can you? Perhaps you both met with Sorensen."

"What are you suggesting?" Kyle's brow rose over an incredulous glare.

Hutch walked around the table to lean his back against the one-way mirror. Mack couldn't see his face, but Hutch's tone suggested he was enjoying himself. Of course, the accusation against Lawrence was another deliberate tactic, intended to put him off balance. From all accounts, it was working.

At the beginning of his investigation, Mack had considered the possibility of Lawrence being involved but dismissed it as too unlikely. At thirty-one, the guy was already rich and well-connected from taking on high-profile legal cases. In all likelihood, he nursed political ambitions. True, he was crazy about Gemma and would do a lot to win her back, but Mack doubted that would stretch to art fraud. He didn't come across as a risk-taker. Quite the opposite.

Hutch lifted a casual shoulder. "You tell me what I'm suggesting."

"Good God! You're not seriously trying to make me a suspect, are you?"

"You were there?"

"Damn you, superintendent. Your superiors will hear about this."

Hutch ignored that threat, just as Mack knew he would. "You would agree that it's all very convenient. Both of you in Venice right before the fake Bonvalet was delivered to McCallister's. Do the math, Mr. Lawrence." Hutch scratched at a gap between two shirt buttons, shrewdly waiting for Kyle to digest the implication, then turned to Gemma.

"Were you with your fiancé the whole time?"

Gemma flicked a glance at Kyle before answering. "Of course."

"Doing what?"

"The usual things. Sightseeing. Eating at restaurants and cafés."

Kyle cleared his throat. "That's not quite true, superintendent." He paused to slide a look at the one-way mirror. "We did what engaged couples normally do. We spent most of the time in our room."

"Oh, that's not—" Gemma started to say and then stopped in confusion. Mack held his breath. It wasn't jealousy that caught him. Or even that Lawrence's words were aimed squarely at him. It was the dismayed look on her face at the lie. Mack couldn't stop his small glimmer of satisfaction that she hadn't covered for the jackass.

Going by his barely contained smirk, Hutch relished this new line of questioning.

"Is that true, Dr. Gilmore? You spent your time at the hotel ... " he paused for emphasis, "doing what engaged couples *do*?"

Her cheeks flamed with embarrassment. "Actually ... " She stopped again, obviously stuck between loyalty to her ex-fiancé and telling the truth.

Hutch moved on, satisfied with the discomfort he'd caused. She was rattled now, staring into her lap and fidgeting with a shirt button.

"Dr. Gilmore ... " Hutch paused, waiting until she looked up. "You know that the painting you authenticated is now back at McCallister's being checked?"

She frowned briefly as she tried to recall. "Yes. John Allen told me."

Hutch pushed his big frame forward and rested his elbows on the table. "Do you know what they found, Dr. Gilmore?"

"No, but I guess you're about to tell me," she answered, her chin rising defiantly. Mack smiled, despite the grimness of the situation. She wasn't about to just give up—not by a long shot.

"The painting is a fake."

Kyle opened his mouth to speak, but Gemma cut in. "But I would have known."

"Exactly right, Dr. Gilmore."

Her eyes widened at the realization of what she'd said. "But—"

"Is there a question here?" Kyle interrupted hastily.

Hutch grinned. "I'm told it's a very good forgery. It might never have been discovered, considering the original is unlikely to turn up. Of course, Sorensen couldn't have done it without your help."

"He *did* do it without my help!" she shot out before Kyle could stop her.

"So you know Sorensen?"

She blinked and turned to Kyle with frantic eyes. "No, I—"

"Let's move on, superintendent," Kyle clipped. "If you have more questions, ask me as, apparently, I'm a suspect in all this."

Hutch walked slowly to the table, sat down, and leaned back to casually straighten his tie over his paunch.

"The thing is, Mr. Lawrence, we don't need your client's confession. Sorensen's statement is enough to arrest her."

"I don't think so," Kyle said quietly. "There'll be no arrest."

"Oh really?" Hutch sounded casual enough, but Mack saw a flicker of uncertainty cross the wily old face. "And what makes you say that?"

"Because, superintendent, within an hour every major news outlet will have the story of how McCallister's, the most prestigious auction house in the country, is up to its esteemed neck in an art fraud case. They'll know how the young and dedicated Dr. Gemma Gilmore was made a scapegoat for their own incompetence. I know who the public will sympathize with."

Mack straightened. Jesus, Lawrence was right. McCallister's was terrified of this coming out. Every conversation he'd had with John Allen discussed the need to keep it quiet.

Gemma turned to Kyle, her expression total surprise. Obviously, this was a last resort tactic she hadn't known about. Even her jackass ex looked unsettled by his own threat. As a high-profile defense lawyer, he'd know better than anyone the damaging effects of publicity.

"Are you sure you want to put your client through a media frenzy?"

Kyle's gaze was steady on Hutch. "My client's career is on hold, her reputation at stake. We have nothing to lose. I suggest you consult McCallister's before doing anything rash." He rose to his feet. "Now, if there's nothing else you want to discuss, we'll be on our way."

Hutch stood as well, clearly caught off-guard. "Is this really how you want to do this, Dr. Gilmore? There'll be no leniency without a confession." When she didn't answer, Hutch walked across to the door and held it open. "You're free to go. For now."

Gemma turned in her chair to look directly at the one-way mirror, and Mack wondered if she could somehow she see him. But then she frowned.

"Is Mack Buchanan here?"

Hutch followed her gaze. "I'm not sure."

"I'd like to speak to him. Alone."

"For God's sake, that's the last person you should have anything to do with," Kyle barked. He started walking to the door. "We're leaving, superintendent."

Gemma sat completely still, her eyes locked on the mirror. "Please get Mr. Buchanan."

Kyle did a fast U-turn and sat down again. "Gem, as your attorney, I'm ordering you not to do this." He took her hand. "They've agreed to release you. We can go."

She pulled her fingers free from Kyle's grip.

"Now. And turn off the microphone."

"I'll check if he's here," Hutch said, banging the door on his way out.

Pacing the length of the office and back again, the old cop glared through the mirror. "Damn, damn, damn. I should've seen that one coming. We can't risk charging her. I'll need to talk to McCallister's before we go any further. In the meantime, she'll have to be released. You want to talk to her? Without Lawrence there, nothing will be admissible in court, but still, she might say something useful."

Mack didn't answer. Talking to her now wouldn't be much use. She didn't trust him an inch.

He watched Kyle frantically talking to Gemma on the other side of the glass. It wasn't difficult to work out their conversation. The jackass would be giving her every reason in the book not to talk to him. By the way she was staring straight ahead, her eyes fixed on the mirror, he obviously wasn't making any headway.

"Do you want to talk to her, Mack?" Hutch asked again.

"Last night, I told her I believed she was innocent," he said, staring down at the floor as if it could throw some light on the whole mess. "So goddamned stupid." More than stupid, he realized now. He'd abandoned every last shred of his common sense just to have her. For the first time in years, Mack felt at a loss. He'd always operated with military precision—identifying potential problems before the impact. Calculating risk, focusing on solutions. Doing what he had to do to get the job done.

But this? How the fuck had it all happened?

"Don't beat yourself up about it, pal." Hutch placed a hand on his shoulder. "So are you going to talk to her or not?"

Crap. He should walk away, just as he always did when he was finished with a woman. Except he wasn't finished with Gemma. He wanted—no, he *needed*—to hear her explanation of why she'd done it. Maybe if she said the words, it would put a stop to what he felt. The wanting her. In a few days, he'd be back to active duty, but it couldn't come soon enough. "Yeah, I'll talk to her. But not here."

"So what do I tell her?"

Mack was halfway through the exit before he answered.

"Tell her I've gone."

CHAPTER TWELVE

"I go on a cruise, and I come back to this. I simply can't believe it."

With a sigh of resignation, Gemma set her fork down and soldered on her best "do we have to talk about it over lunch" face, which meant she was pouting. From her mother's expression, it hadn't worked. Hints—subtle or otherwise—were generally lost on Sally Gilmore.

Her mother's call this morning, summoning Gemma to lunch at Antonio's, was expected. She'd immediately texted her mother with the news following the police interview. Not that she'd wanted to tell her so soon, but there was little point in delaying the unavoidable fallout. Her mother was back in New York and would find out within hours. This way, Gemma could be prepared.

It was typical of her mother to choose a busy restaurant for their meeting. She preferred to have potentially difficult conversations with her daughter on neutral territory, with minimal fuss. As usual, she was impeccably turned out—her chestnut-colored hair swept into a chignon, her perfectly tailored forest-green suit selected to match her green eyes. She barely looked forty-five, ten years below her actual age. Right now, she looked cross, inconvenienced. Gemma didn't think her mother had actually grasped the implication of the fraud accusation.

"Believe it, Mom."

"I dread to think what Lydia Cummings will say about this," her mother continued with a pained expression. She turned to look around the restaurant as if checking for Lydia behind one of the decorative palms set along the walls. "She's the biggest gossip in the bridge club. I'll never be able to hold my head up after this."

Gemma tried not to show her irritation. Nearly every sentence that ever came out of her mother's mouth started with "I."

"You'll be able to handle Lydia and the club. You always do. Tell me about your cruise."

"I won't have you changing the subject, Gemma," she chided. "Tell me how this mess happened."

"As I said, McCallister's has accused me of authenticating a forgery."

"I know *that*. By the way, did you?" Her tone suggested she seriously considered it a possibility.

"Not you as well? The whole world already thinks I'm a criminal. Or at least they will, once this gets out. Kyle has managed to delay the whole thing, but that won't last long. McCallister's will have to press charges."

"I just knew this would happen. Thank goodness you have Kyle. If only—"

Good Lord. Not this again.

"For heaven's sake, Mom," she interrupted sharply, "this has nothing to do with my not marrying Kyle."

Her mother sniffed huffily and took several sparrow-sips of her dry martini before delicately dabbing at the corners of her mouth with a napkin. "I wasn't going to say that. But now that you mention it"—she paused to fold the napkin, and Gemma inwardly groaned, anticipating the next words—"I know as well as you do, Gemma, this would never have happened if you'd married him."

As always, the logic of her mother's statement about Kyle and marriage was a mystery. She decided not to pursue it. That would be a marathon conversation best left for another time.

"The Wentworth went for a record price. It was on the news."

Her mother shrugged away the information, undeterred. "I know your father would have wanted you to marry Kyle."

It wasn't true. Her gentle, kind, so beloved father wouldn't have cared if she'd married a cash-strapped biker covered in tats, provided he was a good man and kind to his daughter. Her father had been her rock growing up—the buffer between her and her mother. Always there, encouraging her to do whatever particular hobby she'd latched onto at the time. He'd been thrilled at her decision to study fine art. She was nineteen when he died from cancer. Oh how she missed him, and never more than right now.

You are all your mother has, he'd reminded her just days before his death. *Be patient with her*.

Yes, she was patient with her mom, even though they didn't see eye-to-eye on some things. Most things, actually. Gemma could never really understand how her parents had found each other—or stayed together, for that matter. Her father had been a highly respected college professor and her mother a high school teacher when they met. Within a week of her marriage, her mother had quit her job to devote herself to being a professor's wife and securing herself on the right social ladder, which neither Gemma nor her father ever understood the point of. But still, she had created a comfortable home, and Gemma had wanted for nothing.

"Dad would want me to be happy, Mom," she answered evenly. "Besides, Kyle is with Miranda now, and I've got more important things to think about."

Sally took another sip of her cocktail while she studied her daughter. Her eyes narrowed as if just becoming aware of something. "You're very pale. Tell me everything about the investigation. Who's leading it?"

At least they were onto another topic, even if it was Gemma's criminal career. "There's an investigator—Mack Buchanan. I'm not exactly sure who he works for, but it must be for McCallister's or Interpol or ... somebody like that," she ended a little lamely.

Just saying his name hurt.

"I assume he thinks you're guilty?"

Gemma closed her eyes against the sharp truth of her mother's words. "Yes."

"I suppose he would. After all, the painting was in your hands."

"Gee, thanks, Mother," she muttered down at her salad. "Actually," she said, looking up defiantly, "just so you know, the painting 'in my hands,' as you put it, was genuine."

"Then convince him."

Good grief, if only it were that simple.

"Don't you think I've tried? I've done nothing but try to convince him." Among other things. She felt a sudden heat curling low in her belly. She crossed her legs. "He thinks I'm a liar. Besides—"

"Besides what?" her mother asked when she faltered.

"Besides, he used me to get what he wanted." That sounded peevish enough for her mother's eyes to widen in surprise.

"My goodness, Gemma. What *is* going on?" Her voice rose in interest. "What did he do?"

"Oh, not much—just lied to me, that's all." She hadn't intended to sound so bitter. It had the effect of opening her mother's mouth to a perfect O.

"I want to know *everything*, Gemma," she half-whispered, leaning across the table as if Lydia might pop up from below with a microphone.

Gemma wondered if, for once, she should tell her everything. If nothing else, it would be interesting to see the reaction. Who knows—her mom might possibly be supportive.

"I met him at the auction when the Bonvalet was sold. Then a month later, when Maxim Stonebridge told me that the painting was a forgery, Mack Buchanan was there. Ever since ... well, he's questioned me over and over. I thought he finally believed me, especially after we"—she stopped briefly as her mother's eyebrows stretched high in surprise—"slept together." She wondered why people used that term when sleeping was the last thing anyone did when they were having sex.

"I must say I'm surprised."

"Are you really?" she asked innocently, playing light with the disapproving tone.

"I assume you liked this man enough to put aside your common sense?"

Gemma blew a very careful, slow breath before responding to the insult. "I guess I did like him."

Did she? Yes, all through their arguments and the scorching sex, she had *liked* Mack and thought he liked her in turn. It was daft thinking on her part. It was just sex to him. Taking what he wanted, then walking away.

That's what hurt the most. His refusal to talk to her at the station. It hadn't been guilt or shame at his actions that made him leave. He'd gone because he was done with her, in every way. In the last forty-eight hours, she'd dialed him on her phone a dozen times to demand answers, only to terminate the call before it connected. She didn't need him to say the hurtful words; she couldn't bear it. When it came down to it, Mack had betrayed her and left her to her fate—that was all the explanation she needed. Knowing the "why" wouldn't ease the wound in her heart.

"You more than like him, don't you?"

The question caught her so off-guard, it took her a few moments to digest its perceptiveness. "No, Mom, I don't 'more than like him.' In fact, I don't want to see or speak to the man ever again."

Her lie lacked conviction, but it went unnoticed.

"I'm glad. Kyle would be devastated."

"Jesus Christ," Gemma whispered.

She picked up the dessert menu, ordering herself to stay calm. Her mother was worse than ever over the whole Kyle thing. "Something chocolate-y would be good." Right now, she needed comfort food, and lots of it.

"You know I don't eat carbs," came the scolding response.

Gemma's phone rang, just as she'd decided on the chocolate sundae topped with hazelnuts. "Gemma Gilmore," she said into the phone, peering around for a waiter among the diners.

"Gemma."

Every cell in her body surged heat in response to the bourbon voice so close to her ear. "Yes," she answered, putting on a "who is this?" tone.

"I need to talk to you."

The nerve of the man.

"Oh, it's you. What would you like to talk about?" She signaled to a waiter as he passed her table. "Chocolate sundae, please. Won't you have a dessert, Mom?"

Her mother pursed her lips as if the question were a social gaffe. "Nothing for me, thank you," she instructed the waiter crisply.

"Actually, this isn't a good time. I have to go," Gemma said into the phone, forcing a casual tone, despite the warmth pooling between her legs. That she could still react in this way, without resistance, was almost unbearable.

"No games, Gemma. I want to talk to you. I'll pick you up later. What time?"

So the arrogance was still there. "You didn't want to talk two days ago."

"What time?"

"Who are you talking to?" her mother chipped in, watching keenly.

"Nobody important, Mom," she answered loudly into the phone. "I don't see what good meeting will do." She'd lost the battle to stay cool. Now she was grumpy.

"Please."

Her heart thudded at the unexpected plea. He'd never said please before. Ever. Curiosity might be rearing its head, but damned if she would make it easy for him.

She let the seconds stretch in a long, nerve-crunching silence. "Alright. Pick me up at four."

"Four. Good."

"What exactly do you want to talk about?" she asked on a rush, now realizing that should have been her first question.

But he'd gone.

She felt a little numb. Closing her eyes, she visualized him standing at her door. Tall, big-shouldered, and maybe with that heart-melting smile that always made her want to climb up his body to taste it. His sexy voice had liquefied her senses. Again.

Her mother's voice interrupted her thoughts. "You aren't *actually* going to eat that?"

Gemma blinked at the chocolate sundae in front of her. "Oh, thank you," she said to the departing waiter. "*Actually*, I am. Are you sure you don't want a dessert?"

Her question was met with a shrewd, inquisitive stare. "Was that Mack Buchanan?"

She filled her mouth with chocolate, using the time to regain her calm. "Yes. Couldn't you tell?" That was sarcastic. Unnecessary.

"I thought you had nothing to say to him."

"Well, apparently he's got something to say to me."

"You know Kyle wouldn't—"

She felt the hairs rise on the back of her neck. This wasn't the time or place for a showdown, but her mother was asking for it. "For fuck's sake, Mom. Leave Kyle out of it. Don't ever mention him again. Got it?"

The sight of her mother straightening in sheer fright was almost comical. She swept a frantic look around the restaurant, no doubt looking for Lydia, before turning back to stare wide-eyed at her daughter with an expression Gemma had never seen on her mother's face before. The woman was gobsmacked.

"You—you swore!" she finally sputtered, accusingly.

Gemma let out a wild, hysterical laugh. Every head in the restaurant turned in their direction. "I wish you could see the look on your face, Mom. My God, my career is in ruins, I've been accused of a $50 million fraud, the investigator has used me for fun, and all you're worried about is my bad language and the well-being of my ex-fiancé. Don't you think that's funny? I do."

Her mother flicked an embarrassed glance around the room before turning back to Gemma. "No ... I—"

"Have you ever thought about what might happen to me? I could go to prison. What would Lydia say then?" Gemma snapped, sobering up fast at the realization that it really could happen.

Her mother turned as white as the tablecloth. Gemma had never realized until now that Lydia's name was a weapon.

"That's ridiculous. They wouldn't do that."

It took all her strength not to laugh again. If she did, she'd completely lose it. "Yes, Mother. They would."

"I can't believe it. If only your father were here."

Gemma shoved her phone in her purse and got to her feet, suddenly tired. "Look, I have to go. I'll call you."

She was three steps from the table when she heard the plaintive voice behind her.

"I'm going to book another cruise, so you needn't worry about me."

Gemma kept walking, resisting the urge to suggest she take Lydia for company.

CHAPTER THIRTEEN

He lived in a loft.

Gemma slowly turned, taking in her surroundings. Astonishing. Not so much the place, but that he'd brought her here. To his inner sanctum. At least, that's what it felt like.

For such a large space, it had surprisingly comfortable, almost cheery warmth with its polished wood floors and brightly patterned oriental rugs. That was also surprising. The place was beautiful. And obviously expensive. At one end, the kitchen gleamed in stainless steel and granite, while at the other, an enormous bed was neatly made up and topped with a colorful mohair throw. Somehow she couldn't quite imagine him coming home to this place after a day's work. But when she thought about it, she couldn't imagine him coming home—period. He just existed. Like in a dream.

He cleared his throat.

She spun toward the sound. She'd been so focused on her surroundings she'd almost forgotten he was standing in silence, waiting for her to complete her assessment of his home. If this was his home. There was no way to tell. He'd barely said two words during the drive across town, other than to remind her to buckle up.

Actually, she shouldn't be here. Not when Kyle had warned her not to talk to McCallister's staff, the police, the media, and—most of all—that Buchanan Bastard. Gemma had been happy to lie low. Besides, she'd already decided, even accepted, that Mack was out of her life and she was out of his. But the promise of answers to her questions was reason enough to ignore Kyle's instructions, surely?

"How long have you lived here?" she asked, taking another, slow, awed 360° turn to study the place yet again. There was very little in the way of furniture—just two luxurious black leather sofas set opposite a smoky-glass coffee table, a gorgeous oak dining set with six chairs, a sideboard, and a bookcase crammed with books. Nothing on the walls for decoration, but the simplicity and sparseness somehow worked to create a sense of tranquility. Knowing more about him only added another layer to the mystery of who he was.

"A while."

Evasive, but she couldn't complain. It was miracle enough that he'd brought her here.

"It's beautiful. This *is* your apartment, isn't it?"

"Did you think I lived with a pool table and a beer fridge?" he answered quietly.

That was tactless on her part. "Oh no, it's just that ... it's just not what I expected.

He sat down and waved a hand toward the sofa opposite. "Please sit down."

His cool tone came as a blunt reminder exactly what he thought of her.

So what? she told herself firmly as she sat down on the soft leather. Protesting her innocence would be a waste of time anyway. Besides, she was here for information. Nothing else.

Gemma arranged her blue floral skirt over her knees and clasped her hands in her lap, aware that he was looking at her legs. Unwanted warmth radiated along her skin. He could arouse her with just a look. It didn't seem fair for a man to have such power.

"Why did you bring me here?" she snapped in irritation, now wondering what had possessed her to agree to come here. Just a few minutes in and he already had her at a disadvantage.

"You wanted to know about me. It's time for total honesty." His eyes glinted. "Don't you think?"

That jab was hard to miss. To hell with him.

"Why are you involved in the investigation?"

"I was asked."

"Inspector Hutchinson?"

"Maybe." He leaned back, and her eyes automatically coasted the length of him. She looked up, hoping he hadn't noticed her staring. Of course he had. That knowing look said it all.

"At the station, why did you want to see me?"

"Simple," she said, drawing a deep breath to put her back on track. "To find out how you could spend the night," her voice quavered at the memory, "knowing what was going to happen."

"I didn't know."

"You're a fucking liar," she spat out, then blinked in shock at her crudeness. His eyes blazed in anger, and Gemma tensed. She knew what he was capable of. He could suddenly throw her over his shoulder, carry her out of his apartment, and dump her in the elevator. Just because he hadn't carried out his threat that day at McCallister's didn't mean he wouldn't do it now.

"That's the third time you've called me a liar. A bit rich coming from you, princess."

He began to rise. Gemma braced herself but kept going, forcing herself to say the words. "You don't care who you hurt. This is all just a game to you, isn't it?"

His eyes narrowed as he sat back down, shading the hazel depths. "Game?" he echoed, as if her question had given him food for thought. He leaned back and crossed his arms, drawing her attention to the thick biceps straining the short sleeves of his black T-shirt. Those arms had secured her so many times. Held her close …

"Okay, tell me three things that you wish were true about yourself. Two truths, one lie."

What? Screw him.

"I'm not here to play your stupid game."

Now the hazel depths mocked her. "I guess the truth is too difficult for you?"

And screw his sarcasm.

"Okay, if we have to go through this silly charade, then I ... " She paused, debating whether to stay or leave. If she stayed, things would only get worse. But if she went, she would leave empty-handed.

She made herself more comfortable on the plush leather while she thought. "I wish I were five ten. I wish I were an artist. I wish I had a tattoo. Will that do?"

"You never wanted to be an artist."

"Oh ... Oh, yes that's right," she stammered, surprised at how easily he'd picked the lie. "I've always wanted to study great works rather than paint."

Heavens, why had she said that? He didn't need to know her wants. She tried to think of something equally devious to ask him.

"Tell me three humiliating moments in your life," she said. This should be good.

He answered without hesitation. "Falling over on stage at a school play. Getting caught having sex on a flight to Cleveland. Puking in the church at my kid brother's wedding."

Easy.

"You didn't throw up at your brother's wedding. What's his name?"

"I did, and his name is Tom. But I never did join the Mile High Club."

She snorted. "I find that hard to believe." *It wouldn't be from lack of offers*, she thought with a stab of irrational jealousy. How silly to resent every woman who had known the pleasure of him. She shouldn't care, so why on earth did she? "Besides, you like taking risks, don't you?" she added huffily.

"That depends." He tapped his fingers on his chin while he studied her, making her look away in embarrassment. He'd read her.

"Three regrets, Doctor."

Oh, she had enough of those swirling around in her past and present, but she wasn't about to give him more ammunition. She chewed at a corner of her mouth while she sifted through all the things she'd wished she hadn't done or said, searching for something safe.

"That I didn't go to Europe after graduation. Not having the courage to ask Manny Stevens out when I was sixteen. Giving up piano lessons."

His response came in a flash. "Manny Stevens."

Heck, he was good.

"True. Manny was a total jerk."

He quirked an eyebrow at that, making her heart lurch at the memory of his teasing when he—

"Tell me *your* regrets," she asked on a rush, pushing the hot memory aside.

"Not being a firefighter. Not staying in touch with childhood friends. Not working so hard."

All lies.

"I thought we were going to be honest?"

His expression flickered acknowledgement. "Not supporting Tom more when we were growing up. Not ... "

"Not what?" she pressed when he hesitated.

"Not being there when my father died."

"Oh," she whispered, surprised at his candor. "And the third?"

"How did you get Sorensen to do the forgery?"

The question came with such directness it took her a moment to answer. "I ... I didn't."

Eyes as cold as a winter frost caught hers. Held her fast. "He's the best, apparently. You must have promised him millions. "

This was dangerous territory. She needed to leave. But how to make an exit without it looking like he'd got the better of her?

"We all know there are forgers out there. Once they're caught, their names become common knowledge." Oh, to hell with explanations. She sprang to her feet. "I have to—"

"Sit down, Gemma."

She sat down, irritated by the way her body warmed under the order. "I've told you again and again, I don't know any forger!"

"Off the record, tell me the truth."

How could anyone convince the inconvincible?

"I *am* telling you the truth!" she insisted anyway. "I don't know him. I've never met him. Why can't you believe that?"

His eyes drilled hers. "Everything you say stays between us."

"This is ridiculous!" She leapt up and walked across to one of the floor-to-ceiling windows that spanned the outer walls of the loft. Resting her forehead against the glass, she stared at the traffic below and the pedestrians clustered at intersections, waiting to cross. To her left, Central Park lay in the distance—a welcoming oasis of green. Oh, to be Tinkerbelle and fly to that haven right now.

He was beside her. For a big man, he could move so quietly.

"In his confession, Sorensen said you met him in Venice at your hotel."

"That's not true. I—" Gemma stopped. Actually, there *had* been someone. An American in the hotel bar. He'd started a conversation with her and Kyle. But he'd only talked about his holiday in Venice. In fact, he hadn't shown any interest in either of them, let alone ask questions about art or where she worked. She couldn't even remember if he'd introduced himself, but he definitely hadn't asked for their names. But there couldn't be any connection, and mentioning some unknown tourist would be tantamount to a confession in Mack's mind. He'd assume there was more to tell.

"Go on?" he urged, leaning close enough for her to be aware of every inch of him. Gemma pushed her cheek to the cool glass. This was so crazy. He was her enemy.

"There was no one," she whispered, closing her eyes as if the futile action could spirit her away from her nemesis.

"I see."

His disbelieving tone said it all: He would never believe her. Gemma braced herself for the next, inevitable question.

She felt his breath skimming her hair when it came. "Whose idea was it to forge the Bonvalet?"

Damn him. Spinning round, she almost fell forward against him. Straightening, she looked up to match his icy gaze. "No one! Tell me your last regret." Not that she wanted to know any more. She just felt slightly sick and needed to go home.

"I think you know."

Resentment simmered and exploded. "Yes, I know. You regret me. Well, I regret you," she shouted, wanting to push him away from her, but uncertain what he might do. "You ... you bastard!"

His mouth compressed to a hard line, and Gemma knew she'd gone too far. She shrank back, expecting the worst.

Angry eyes glittered and locked on hers.

"I regret that I believed you, Gemma. All those goddamned lies. Why couldn't you have trusted me? It didn't need to play out this way."

What a joke. "Is that another trick to get me to confess?" she jeered, no longer caring what he did. Edging away from him, her back hit the glass. "Well, I have another regret, Mack Buchanan." Tears welled but she gulped them down. She was going to say this. "More than anything in my whole life, I regret that you ever *touched* me."

It wasn't true. She might regret her foolishness, but Mack hadn't done anything she hadn't wanted. Yes, he'd pushed all her buttons like no other man, but he was good at that. At sex. So really, there was no reason to beat herself up about wanting him. It wasn't as if she actually cared for him or anything.

His eyes burned with anger. Gemma slid sideways along the glass, suddenly desperate to escape the source of her misery, but he set his palms flat against the pane, blocking her in. Telltale heat flooded her face at the closeness. He'd know. He always did.

"Let me go, Perses. Haven't you caused enough destruction?"

She felt her chin fastened in his big hand, lifted up. Bending low, he kissed her hard until she moaned with need. Oh God, she wanted him.

As if hearing her plea, Perses lifted her skirt with one hand and used the other to ease her legs apart. She felt him work the crotch of her panties aside, his fingers seeking her opening. She shuddered as two fingers sank deep into her body. There would be no teasing this time. No drawing out the pleasure.

He dropped to his knees, and right there, with her backed up against the glass, he shoved her skirt up into her hands, tore apart the crotch of her panties, and, using his thumbs to open her, licked her.

She stood there trembling and clutching at her skirt, spellbound by the sight of his dark head between her legs. She felt his tongue circle her clit and couldn't stop herself from spreading her legs wider, whimpering like a puppy as he blew warm air on her before sinking into her again.

When his tongue thrust into her core, she cried out at the wild, unrestrained invasion. Oh God, it felt incredible. She was fixed to his mouth. She couldn't move. Anyone in the high-rise building behind them could be watching. The thought made it surreal. Dangerous. Hot.

"Oh God," she gasped as his tongue grazed along her sex before dipping into her body again. Gemma was now so dizzy with the intimate sensation her legs couldn't support her. "I can't ... "

With barely a pause, he lifted one leg over his shoulder, then the other. With her back hard to the glass, she was perched on his broad shoulders, her sex spread wide for his mouth. He gripped her butt and reclaimed her, sliding his tongue deep.

She was powerless. Completely open to him and at his mercy. The knowledge heightened the sensation. She squirmed, and he gripped her harder to keep her still. His mouth worked every part of her sex, every lave of his tongue radiating ripples of pleasure along her skin.

Her body coiled. Tightened. Oh God, she was going to come, right here for the whole world to see. Gemma tried to hold back, suddenly embarrassed at the thought of a hundred eyes watching them, but he'd zeroed on her clit again, now relentlessly steering her over the precipice.

She screamed as her orgasm slammed her. Her head fell back against the glass with a loud thump. He paused to look up at her, then, apparently satisfied that she hadn't knocked herself out, bent to her again, finishing her off with slow, languorous strokes that left her quivering.

"I want you inside me," she whispered down to him.

Quietly, without fuss or words, he lifted her into his arms and carried her to the biggest bed she'd ever been on in her life. Snuggled back into the mohair throw, she watched him undress, her eyes automatically finding the raw scar on his side.

"Mack," she murmured, as he lay down beside her. "Please tell me who you are, really?"

But her question was lost in his kiss.

• • •

Mack thrust himself into her again and again. He worried he was hurting her with his deep strokes, but every time he eased off, she dug her fingernails into his back and pumped her hips in frustration.

He slipped his hand under her butt, lifting her hips to him, groaning with lust when she writhed into his hand. Sex had been the last thing on his mind when he'd brought her here. All he wanted was to know why she'd done it. For his own satisfaction, he needed the answer to "why." Was it the money? The danger? The thrill of knowing she could play a joke on the art world and get away with it?

Jesus, he should have known this would happen. They didn't exactly have a hands-off track record. They only had to be in the same room for it to happen.

He buried his face in her scented hair, feeling her breath huffing against his throat with every downward drive. Mack steeled himself against the urge to come. He was hungry for her, and he wanted it to last. She was an intoxicating cocktail of beauty and sensuality and something else that he'd never been able to define. Like a delicate spice with a name forever out of reach. He concentrated on his movements to blank his mind of everything but filling her. Dammit, none of it mattered. He was where he wanted to be, and that was enough.

He slid out of her, feeling her small huff of complaint against his neck.

"Roll over." She flipped onto her stomach and arched her butt up to him, resting her face on the pillow. So fucking sexy. He fitted himself inside her again, holding still to savor the sensation of her wet warmth wrapped around him. Curving his hands around her hips, he pumped her again, more gently now, watching her luscious ass flex in time with his thrusts. In this position, he was so deep inside her that she must be stretched to the limit. He slowed again to give her some respite. A lie. If he kept up this pace, he'd come—but he hadn't had his fill of her. Slipping his hand under her, he rubbed her clit. She jerked forward at the contact, sliding off his cock, moaning loudly at the loss of him. Impaling her again, he touched her more carefully, gently stroking her as he took his own slow pleasure. He was back in control. But damn, she tested his staying power.

She pushed herself back on his shaft, trying to take more of him into her body even though he was balls deep.

"Harder," she whispered.

"I don't want to hurt you."

"Harder," she instructed again. Mack clenched his jaw and gripped her hips to drive deeper, doing his damnedest to be gentle.

"Yes, yes," she breathed.

They were drenched in sweat, each riding their own ferocious wave towards climax. Mack reached down to touch her clit again, but she was already there, stroking herself, so he covered her hand with his own, groaning when she gripped his finger and used it to pleasure herself.

Mack felt her core squeezing his cock. From the way she was wildly rubbing his finger over herself, she was ready to come. It was the green light he needed. Now he let himself go, his rhythm fast and deep, loving her tiny pants of exertion as she arched her butt to meet him at every stroke. She cried out, and Mack's rhythm faltered as ecstasy consumed him.

Mack was shaking by the time he finally came to a stop, but even then, he wanted the sensation of her to last. Sitting back on his haunches, he pulled her with him, settling her into the saddle of his hips, savoring the feel of her sensuous warmth. She lay quiet, her face still resting on the pillow. Their tornado of passion was over. Sated. It should have felt good, but he felt as if a hollow had been gouged in his chest, leaving only emptiness.

"Mack." The muffled sound came so softly it took him a moment to realize that she'd said his name.

"Are you okay?"

She shook her head into the pillow. "No."

He froze. Christ, was she crying? He leaned forward to push the curtain of dark hair away from her face, but he couldn't tell what she was doing with her hand scrunching the pillow up against her cheek. Sliding out of her, he turned her over. Tears streamed down her face, and his heart tore. "Come here." He gathered her up in his arms, tucking her face into his shoulder. "I know you're scared about the case, Gemma."

"It's not that," she blubbered.

"Then what?"

She didn't answer. He could feel her damp cheek against his skin as she wept. He gently massaged her back. Truth was, he didn't know what else to do. She had him in knots.

"Can't you tell me?"

She shook her head into his shoulder. He eased her away so he could see her face, but she nestled into him again, still weeping, so he held her and waited.

"I lied, Mack."

He held his breath. "About what?"

"I don't regret that you touched me."

Good to know, but not exactly the words he'd hoped to hear. "That's a relief," he sighed. "Fucking each other seems to be what we do best."

Was that a sniffle or a giggle?

"Do you think anyone saw us at the window?"

Mack barked a rough laugh. "Probably. Your scream would've woken up the whole block."

She lifted her head to look at him with solemn eyes. Even red-eyed and cherry-nosed and hiding her secrets, she could still captivate him. "That's your fault," she sniffed.

"Is that right? How's your head?"

"Fine." Her face went back to his shoulder.

Yeah, she was a glorious creature. And vulnerable. In the next few days, all hell would break loose. Hutch had briefed him. Lawrence's threat to go to the media had only delayed the inevitable. Mack curled his fingers in her dark hair. If only she would confide in him, he might be able to help her.

He decided to give it one last try. Grasping her hair, he eased her head back. "Talk to me, Gemma. Tell me what you're thinking right now."

She looked at him, her blue eyes searching his, and he thought she was finally about to open up. But then the blue clouded, and she turned her head away. "I have to go. Kyle gave me orders not to discuss the case."

She wouldn't talk. And it wasn't just the jackass's orders that kept her silent. She didn't trust him, and it hurt.

"Get dressed. I'll take you home," he growled, lifting her away from him. He hadn't intended to sound harsh, but it was probably better this way. Slipping off the bed, he removed the condom and dragged on his jeans and T-shirt, waiting for her to dress.

Taking his keys from the coffee table, Mack picked up her panties. "You'll want these," he said, holding out the flimsy, ripped lace.

She put them in her bag. They both stood awkwardly, neither knowing what to say.

Mack walked her to the door. Pulling it open to let her pass, he waited while Gemma turned to gaze around the apartment, as if memorizing the place. She wouldn't be back. This was their swansong, and they both knew it. In two days, he would leave for his next undercover assignment.

By then, Gemma would be under arrest.

CHAPTER FOURTEEN

"Honestly, I'm fine on my own."

Why hadn't she suggested going to his place? Even if Kyle misinterpreted that as a "let's get back together" gesture, at least she could have left when she was ready. Now she was stuck with him in her apartment. Okay, that was mean. The poor guy had been dragged away from an important meeting to save her sorry ass from spending a night in jail.

The police had arrested her early that morning, followed by an appearance before a judge six hours later. Kyle had performed like a star, successfully arguing for bail despite the prosecution's contention that Gemma was a flight risk, especially with $50 million waiting to be claimed.

So, here she was. Back home, safe and sound.

With Kyle.

"You really don't need to stay, you know," she tried again, feeling guilty for wanting to be alone. Would it be too ungracious to fake tiredness as an excuse to escape to her bed? Yes, it would, she scolded herself. For all Kyle's lecturing to stay away from Mack, and his disgust when she hadn't, he was still standing by her.

She watched him carefully measure two spoons of coffee into the French press, then fill it to the brim with boiling water. Okay, she'd give him two hours and then fake tiredness. After all, it was true enough. She needed to take a shower and go to bed.

Strange to think that Mack had stood in that exact same spot a few days ago, fixing her breakfast. Kyle pulled two mugs from the cupboard and checked them for coffee stains. Gemma sighed. He was so fastidious.

"You shouldn't be alone, Gem. Besides, there's a lot to go over. We have a defense to prepare."

That wasn't the real reason Kyle had insisted on driving her home and coming up. The trial had to be months away. No, he was here to talk about Mack and why she'd gone to his apartment. Why she would involve herself with a man like that? She didn't know herself, let alone how to explain it to him.

"How bad is it?" she asked, pouring the coffees and sliding onto a stool. Of course it was bad. As bad as it got. Her career was history, regardless of the outcome. No auction house would touch her after this.

Kyle sat on the stool next to her and added milk to his coffee. "I won't lie to you. It will be tough to convince a jury that you thought the Bonvalet was real. Not after the prosecution's witnesses testify to your expertise." He laughed dryly. "I'd have to show you were incompetent, and your track record says otherwise. Besides, with Sorensen's testimony ... well, it won't be easy."

"But he's lying."

"That'll be hard to prove. He knew about our trip to Venice. The name of the hotel. All of it. Besides, the prosecutor will say Sorensen has no reason to lie."

"So why has he?"

Kyle tested his coffee and added more milk. "I'll put the firm's top investigator on it. Sorensen has implicated you for a reason. We just need to figure out what it is."

"You know that American tourist who spoke to us in the hotel bar?"

Kyle frowned while he sipped his coffee. "Yeah. Said he'd been on a gondola ride or something. What about him?"

"Could it have been Sorensen?"

"Possibly. Why do you ask?"

She tried to ignore his suspicious look.

"Oh nothing. I just thought there might be a connection."

Kyle's tone switched to lawyer mode. "Tell me, who put the idea into your head?"

"No one," she answered, feeling her cheeks warm under his hard stare.

"No one by the name of Buchanan?"

"Okay, well ... yes. He said Sorensen was at the hotel, that's all. I thought of the tourist. It's probably nothing."

Kyle's mug went down with a small thud. "What did you tell him?"

"I didn't tell him about the tourist, if that's what you mean."

"Thank God for that. Buchanan tried to set you up. He'd say you confessed to meeting Sorensen." He dragged his hand over his head, and Gemma noticed for the first time how strained he looked. "What in God's name possessed you go to his apartment, anyway?"

Crunch time. The conversation she'd dreaded.

"He said he wanted to talk. I thought he might tell me something useful."

"In other words, he lured you."

Had he? It hadn't taken much in the way of luring to get her there.

"It wasn't like that."

"So what was it like?"

"He lives in a loft," she said, deliberately misunderstanding him. "We talked about his decorating." Decorating? Good Lord, couldn't she think of something better than that? "It's on the top floor of a twenty-story apartment block," she added unnecessarily.

When in a hole, stop digging, Gemma.

"Really," he said dryly. "Anything more to add?"

The hole got bigger.

"Oh ... well, it has leather sofas and beautiful oriental rugs."

"And the bed?"

"It's enormous. Oh, for goodness' sake, Kyle, it was nothing. I came straight home as soon as I realized he wasn't going to talk."

This was worse than explaining to her mother why she was home late from school.

"At first, I thought your behavior was some kind of transgression." He paused to let the word hang in the air between them like the sword of Damocles. "But now I can see that you actually care for that bastard. Do you?"

"No!" She set her own coffee mug down firmly. "How could I?" she added, as if her question could make the truth untrue. Sure, she loved his body, but hell, any woman would love that. Actually caring about him would make her the biggest fool in the world. "He was just good at—"

"Sex?" Kyle queried, his eyebrows floating high.

Too late to rephrase.

"That's not what I meant. I was going to say, 'at tricking me.'" How ridiculous and weak that sounded. "So tell me," she rushed on, to get off the subject, "where is Sorensen now?"

"Still in Venice, awaiting extradition. That'll take several months. At least it buys time for us." Kyle stared into his coffee.

"Kyle, maybe someone else should represent me on this case."

He shook his head in answer, still looking down.

"Under the circumstances, don't you think it would be best?" she urged. "You have other cases."

His hand went up to silence her protest. "I'm your attorney, no arguments."

"So what happens now? I mean with the trial?"

"There'll be a hearing, and a trial date set." He looked up, his blue eyes seeking hers. "I forgive you, Gem."

"Forgive?" she echoed, puzzled but at the same time dreading what was about to say.

"For being with him. You've been under so much stress, so I can understand how you'd get carried away." He smiled sadly. She didn't know what to say, so she stayed silent.

"After all," he continued, "I thought I loved Miranda."

Gemma slowly slipped off her stool and walked around the counter to put her mug in the dishwasher. Leaning back against the edge of the sink, she crossed her arms and stared at the floor.

"Kyle, whatever you think—"

"Marry me, Gem."

Her head snapping up and her mouth hanging open must have looked like a *yes* to Kyle because his face suddenly lit up. "A small ceremony and Paris or London for a honeymoon. Anywhere you want."

He was halfway around the counter with his arms out before Gemma found words.

"And Miranda?" she spluttered.

"She moved out." He actually smirked with his news.

"How convenient."

He didn't seem to notice her sarcasm, or he didn't care. "Under the circumstances, I didn't think you'd want a big wedding. You *are* facing a serious criminal charge, after all. Something discreet would be best. For both our sakes."

"Gee, it's a wonder you want to marry me at all," she muttered.

That only widened his smirk.

"That's the thing. I don't care. I just want you."

Good grief. He was really serious about this. From his expression, Kyle obviously expected her to throw herself into his arms.

"But I don't want you," was all Gemma could think of to say.

Kyle's eyes rounding in bewilderment would have been comical in any other situation. He looked like a child denied an ice cream at the movies.

"I know it's not exactly good timing, so take a couple of days to think about it."

Gemma rammed home the message. "It's over," she said, flinching at her bluntness. Kyle's backhanded proposal might be clumsy and thoughtless, but at one time, she'd been more than happy to accept his offer. "Kyle, I don't want to hurt you. I'll always be fond of you, respect you, and be your friend if you need me, but it can't be like it was."

Heavens, that sounded so cliché.

"Of course, this will disappoint your mother."

She had never realized until that moment how manipulative Kyle was. "My mother has nothing to do with this."

He looked at her, almost pityingly. "She told me that after your father died, she despaired that you'd ever find the right man."

Gemma rolled her eyes. "The right man being wealthy?"

Kyle looked slightly uncomfortable, but it didn't stop him or even slow him down. "I can give you everything you could possibly need, Gem. As my wife, you'll be there to support my career. Who knows, you could end up the wife of a governor."

He looked so proud of himself she could only shake her head. "I don't believe this."

"But I can look after you. You know that." His brow wrinkled in confusion.

When he reached for her, she stepped away. "No. I don't believe what I'm hearing. I think you'd better leave."

He didn't move, so she stalked past him toward the door. "Now would be good."

"You think Buchanan is going to come back, don't you? Yeah, he'll be back all right. As a witness for the prosecution."

She froze on the spot, barely breathing as Kyle's words sunk in. Words said in spite, but that didn't make them any less true. When Mack had dropped her off at her apartment two days ago, she'd assumed he wouldn't be back. Never had it crossed her mind that he might testify in court against her.

"But ... " Gemma had to stop for a moment to think. "But surely he can't do that. I mean he's a government agent or something. Would they let him testify?"

"He's a threat," Kyle answered ambiguously, walking over to her to slip an arm around her shoulders, drawing her to him. "But don't worry about Buchanan. I can deal with him." He pulled her closer. His body felt strange to her now. Cold and uninviting.

"The thing is, Gem," he continued, squeezing her shoulder, "you need looking after." He ducked his head to look at her, and she recoiled at his patronizing smile.

Wrenching herself from his hold, Gemma pulled opened the door. "Goodbye, Kyle."

Kyle stood in the doorway, not moving. "You'll realize how much you need me when Buchanan comes back." When Gemma didn't respond, he stepped into the passage, turning to fire a parting shot.

"That bastard will ruin everything for you."

No. Mack had already done that.

• • •

She showered, changed into jeans and a blouse, and took a cab to the Enright. It was late afternoon, but she still had an hour before closing. This had been her most precious place when she wasn't working. Now it felt like a sanctuary.

At this time of the day, most of the exhibition rooms had emptied out of visitors, so she had the place more or less to herself. Now that she was quite alone, she felt much better.

Gemma walked slowly from room to room, stopping to study her favorite paintings. Every room had at least one work to linger over.

Walking into the Augustin room, she paused to look at the nude that Mack had studied, or at least had pretended to study and then declared passable. Actually, it was the best of Augustin's women. *Perhaps he's not such a philistine after all.*

That day, she'd tried to teach him a lesson. Instead, he'd given her a lesson in lovemaking.

She shook off the memory. Mack was gone, and if he ever did come back, it would probably be to see her sent to jail. Kyle had warned her it would be a difficult case, and he wasn't exaggerating. If nothing else, he was a consummate legal professional.

Gemma had never realized until now how mismatched she and Kyle were. She'd never doubted that he loved her and would "look after" her, as he so condescendingly put it. But all through their engagement, he'd never once suggested she give up her career. But looking back, she should have seen it. Kyle had only ever talked about *his* career and *his* ambitions.

Still, Kyle was no longer her concern. She had a trial to worry about and the business of finding another lawyer to represent her, although she doubted that Kyle would allow that. If anything, his hatred for Mack would make him even more determined to secure a not guilty verdict for her.

"Gemma."

She nearly jumped out of her skin at the soft voice close behind her. Spinning around, she saw it was Jamie, his green eyes smiling.

"God, Jamie," she yelped, slapping a hand over her heart. "You scared the life out of me, creeping up like that."

"Sorry. We thought you'd be here."

"We?" she asked, looking past Jamie to the empty doorway.

He grinned. "Lucy's outside, arguing with the cab driver over the fare. She'll be here in a minute."

"Shouldn't you be at work, Jamie O'Mara?" Gemma asked in mock sternness, then laughed when he looked discouraged. "Hey, I'm just kidding. I'm not your boss anymore."

"You'll always be my boss," he retorted, grinning again.

"Anyway, how did you know I'd be here?"

He shook his head as if the question was ridiculous. Lucy's habits were obviously rubbing off on her new boyfriend.

"Gem, you *always* come here on your days off."

"Okay, silly question. Then *why* are you here?"

"We've got news," he announced, his broad grin bunching his cheeks high.

"Oh. Have you and Lucy ... ?" She stopped, not wanting to get it wrong and embarrass him with a question about their relationship. But from his pleased expression, they'd obviously made some momentous decision. "So, how's work?"

"I'm not allowed to tell you."

"Oh. I understand. With everything that's going on, the office must be in lockdown."

Jamie was still grinning like a Cheshire cat, so she walked over to study one of the Augustin's. Jamie followed, standing next to her, his barely contained excitement making her nervous. What the hell was up with him? It couldn't be work because he wasn't allowed to talk about that.

"Okay, Mr. O'Mara," she said briskly, to give him something to do other than grin at her. "What's the first thing you would look for when authenticating this painting?"

Jamie stuck his neck out in the direction of the painting, his grin briefly replaced by a frown of concentration. "Common elements in Augustin's works."

"Absolutely right. And what is the most obvious one?"

Jamie got a mischievous look when he straightened and looked at her. "They're all nudes, right?"

Gemma laughed and then felt sad. Mack would have made a remark like that. "Anything else?"

"GG, you won't believe it!"

Lucy burst into the room. In her scarlet and yellow dress, she reminded Gemma of a fireball that had just been shot out of a cannon.

"Shh, not so loud, Lucy," Jamie scolded, taking charge. "This is an art museum, so you must be quiet."

He turned to Gemma, his face a picture of seriousness. "She's got something to tell you." Lucy had come to a breathless stop beside him and stared at him adoringly.

"Okay, you can tell her now," he said, his earnest expression melting into a warm grin. Gemma couldn't help but envy their happiness.

"The thing is, GG." Lucy dragged in a breath as if her words were stuck in her throat. She sucked in another breath, then another. Finally, she worked a curl into the corner of her mouth. Oh hell, whatever Lucy had to say, it would be big.

"Hurry up, Lucy," Jamie urged.

"The thing is, GG," Lucy began again, stopping to brush the curl from her mouth, "it's not you!"

"What's not me?"

"The Bonvalet, silly. It was switched!" Lucy raised her shoulders and released them again with a happy sigh. "So there it is."

"What Lucy's trying to tell you is that on the morning of the auction, the Bonvalet was removed from the temporary frame and replaced with the forgery," Jamie explained carefully, earning him another adoring look from his girlfriend.

Gemma felt the room start to spin around her. "How—"

"And," Lucy cut in, her face shining, "he confessed."

"Who?" Gemma asked, trying to get the room under control.

Lucy's expression took on her familiar impatience. "The forger, of course!"

"Yes," Gemma said slowly, "we know that."

"No, I mean he confessed about who helped him."

"Yes," Gemma repeated more slowly, wondering if love had turned Lucy's brain to mush. "We know that, too. He said it was me."

"No, silly."

"Hurry up and tell her," Jamie said sternly.

"It was old Rainey!"

When Gemma looked blank, Lucy poked her in the arm. "Rainey, the auctioneer. They found out it was him. Apparently, he offered Sorensen millions to say it was you. The thing is, Gem, you'll never guess who solved it."

"Who?" she asked weakly.

Jamie nudged Lucy's arm. "Tell her."

Lucy clapped her hands in delight. "He went to Venice and got Sorensen to confess everything!"

"Who did?" she asked again.

"Big Mack, of course. I told you that guy was a spy or something."

CHAPTER FIFTEEN

Gemma met him at the Vanderbilt Gate in Central Park. She was half an hour late.

He was standing in front of the iron railing next to the gate, shifting on his feet and looking around with a worried frown. Judging by his relieved expression, he must have thought she wasn't coming. Heavens, who could have the strength to stand him up? In his faded jeans and black T-shirt, his jacket hooked on a thumb and slung over his shoulder, he was as gorgeous as ever.

"Thank God, it stopped drizzling," she said, shaking the rain off her umbrella as she came to a stop beside him. "Have you been waiting long?" A silly, awkward question, considering he'd probably stood on that same spot the whole time getting damp.

"I was here early. How are you?" His mouth turned up in a soft smile, but it seemed sad. She'd didn't think she'd ever seen him sad. Whenever they'd been together, he was either teasing her, loving her, or arguing with her.

"I'm fine. I was a block from my apartment waiting to cross, and it started to drizzle so I had to go back," she explained, holding up the umbrella as if she needed to prove it. "Then I couldn't find a cab, so I walked the whole way. That made me late."

Hell, stop babbling, Gemma.

"No problem. Thank you for meeting me."

"Have you been to the garden before?" She sounded so stiff and formal, but maybe it was better this way. She wasn't here for pleasantries, although exactly what they were here for wasn't clear either.

"Only once, years ago." His gaze swept over her. "You look nice."

"Oh, thanks," she said carelessly, determined to play this whole scene as if she had already moved on and her agreeing to meet him was simply a courtesy. But she couldn't deny that she liked his compliment. Her strappy wedges, white Capri pants, and blue tank top were a reliable any-occasion outfit for when she wasn't sure what to expect, which definitely fit today.

"So do you—look nice, I mean. So when did you get back from Venice?"

"Late last night. I wanted to call you, but I thought you might have gone to bed. Would you like to walk or sit or go for coffee or something?"

He was nervous—she hadn't expected that from the most self-assured man on the planet. "Why don't we walk?" she suggested.

He nodded.

While she folded up her umbrella and stowed it in her tote bag, he slipped on his jacket, and together they walked through the huge wrought-iron gateway and along one of the paths flanked with flowers in full summer bloom. That he'd suggested this place to meet was a surprise. Perhaps he wanted to show her a romantic side. But he looked more preoccupied than romantic, with his hands deep in his pockets, his gaze fixed on the path ahead of them.

They walked for a good five minutes in total silence, both of them seemingly stuck for something to say. There were few people about, but it was late afternoon, and the rain would have kept most visitors away.

She stopped to look at a display of white petunias next to a park bench.

He seemed to take that as a cue. "Perhaps we should sit for a while."

Gratefully, she sank down on a dry spot on the seat, relieved that he'd suggested it before she'd had to. Her wedges weren't designed for long walks, and in her rush, she'd tied the fabric ankle straps too tight for comfort.

Now she felt as nervous as he did. He was so different today, unsure of himself.

She leaned down and busied herself with loosening the straps on her shoes, aware he was watching her fingers clumsily retying the bows. Finally, when her nerves had settled and her shoes were comfortable enough for more walking, she sat back up and waited for him to speak.

Except all he did was lean forward to rest his forearms on his big thighs, staring at the cobblestones beneath his feet. Dammit, it was his invitation to meet, so he could at least start the ball rolling. She waited it out, using the time to study him: the fine shape of his head under the dark, ultrashort haircut, the handsome profile, and the thick, masculine neck with the small swell of Adam's apple. He was so beautiful, and he had been hers, for a while.

"I was an asshole, Gemma."

Her heart lurched at the unexpected burst of words, not to say the frankness of the confession. She opened her mouth to speak, but when he swallowed hard and dropped his head a little, she closed it and waited again.

"I should have believed you when you told me you didn't do it." He looked up and gazed into the distance, then turned to her with quiet eyes. "I'm sorry for that. Deeply sorry."

"You were just doing your job, weren't you?" She wasn't excusing him—couldn't excuse him. Beautiful or not, apologetic or not, he'd hurt her heart more than anyone in her entire life. It wasn't even accidental, the kind of hurt where things happen beyond someone's control, and all anyone can do is accept it for what is. No, this hurt was caused by someone who knew it would lead to pain, but did it anyway.

By the way he flinched, he understood. "Yeah, my job?" he said bitterly. He shook his head in disgust. "Jesus, I set you up to be caught in the safe."

"You must have known I was too clever to fall for that." She hadn't intended to sound flip, but when he smiled sadly, she found herself smiling with him.

They sat in silence again. Perhaps she should suggest coffee after all. Or just get up and say, "Thank you for the walk but I have to go."

"Gemma." The sound of her name said so forcefully made her blink in fright. "There's something I need you to know. For my sake. That night when I stayed in your apartment, I didn't know the forger had named you as his accomplice."

The way he said the words, so determinedly, she could almost believe him.

"How can I know that when you wouldn't see me at the station? You didn't even give me a chance."

"I thought you were guilty."

She should have been angry at the blunt admission, but instead she felt a sharp stab of curiosity. He wasn't making excuses or apologies. He wasn't even trying to fix things. He was being totally honest.

"Then why did you go to Venice?" This was the most important question she had ever asked him.

"Well, someone had to sort the whole fucking thing out."

He was being evasive, and not for the first time. But she was determined now. "But *why* did you go? You didn't have to."

For what seemed liked an eternity, he said nothing. He just sat there, staring into the distance, as quiet and still as one of the concrete statues in the garden. She'd assumed that Interpol had sent him. But his silence suggested there was much more.

Finally, he looked at her. "I had to try and help you. No, that's only part of it. I needed to do it to help me. To stop the guilt."

She held her breath.

"That day at my apartment, it made me realize how much I've used my job to hide. To keep everything in. God, Gemma, it was easy to make love to you, but impossible to tell you how I felt." He ground out a laugh. "It's ironic, really. My work undercover has been a shield for my whole life."

He went silent again. She had so many questions, but she sat quietly, not wanting to risk shutting him down. This was the man she knew almost nothing about laying himself bare.

"I've been doing this work for nine years, since I was twenty-three. Most guys don't last more than four before being reassigned to other work. If they survive, that is."

"Oh God, what are you talking about?"

He met her gaze without blinking. She saw it then. The reality of his life. His job. Who he was.

"You were right when you guessed military intelligence. I work for the government—a small unit that does high-risk undercover work in ... well, various places. Officially, we don't exist. That's all I can tell you."

"Mack," she breathed. "The scar ... ?"

"I got careless," He forced a rough chuckle. "Damned near killed me."

"And the man who did it?" she asked, afraid of the answer, knowing it would be bad.

He looked at her steadily. "Do you really want to know?"

"No." She felt a little numb in the face of his honesty. "Why do you do it?"

His shrugged a shoulder. "I wanted to help keep my country safe. At first that's all it was, along with ... well, thriving on the danger." A darkness came over his features, and she knew whatever he was about to tell her was at the core of his story. "Then my father was killed in a head-on crash with a drunk driver. I was deep undercover and didn't find out for two months. Dad lived for three days and asked for me again and again, and I wasn't there. Can you believe it? Your own father dies, and you go about your life thinking he's alive and well, that when you get home, you'll go see him. Well, after that, I wrapped my life around my job, taking on the toughest assignments. Being the best. It was my way of dealing with the guilt."

His shoulders rose as he took a deep breath, and Gemma drew her own. He had probably never said those words to anyone.

"No, Mack," she said, slipping her hand over his, gripping his fingers. "You can't punish yourself. It wasn't your fault. You didn't know."

He glanced down at her hand on his. "So you see, leaving you was another guilt I couldn't bear."

It was as if he hadn't heard her. She wanted desperately to put her arms around him, but she held back, sensing he didn't want comfort. Not yet.

"Tom is a good man. He's turned out well."

"And your mom?"

"She died of a heart condition when I was ten."

"Oh Mack, I'm sorry."

"Don't be. Tom and I had a good life growing up. Our dad was great. A military man, like me. Maybe he would've understood.

"Do you have to do it? Your job, I mean?" It wasn't really her business to ask, but suddenly it mattered more to her than anything in her own life ever could.

His hand slid from under hers to tuck a stray tendril of her hair back from her face. She leaned into the warm touch.

"At the moment I have no choice. It's not the kind of work where you can say 'I quit' and then walk out the door. What about you? Are you going back to McCallister's?"

She was so distracted by everything he'd told her, she had to think. "I don't know. They apologized and asked me to go back.

I think they're terrified Kyle will go to the media with a tell-all if they don't take me back."

"How is the jackass, by the way?"

"No idea. He left in a huff the last time I saw him. I don't want him," she said firmly.

"Oh."

"Can I ask you something?" she said on an impulse. "Inspector Hutchinson wouldn't tell me anything because the case is ongoing, but was it Sorensen who talked to Kyle and me at the hotel in Venice?"

"Yeah. Rainey set it up as a backup plan. When the forgery was discovered, he offered Sorensen an extra $10 million to say it was you if he was caught. And when he was, he did just that. He was going to jail anyway. Might as well have an extra $10 million waiting on the outside."

"But how did you get Sorensen to confess to all that?"

"Just persuasion," came his answer on a shrug.

She eyed him suspiciously. "I know how you persuade." When he didn't answer, she nudged his arm, pleased that she'd made him smile. "Tell me, Perses."

He laughed then. "Dr. Gilmore, you're not implying I did something inappropriate, are you? Okay, I stood over the guy. Just a little. All legit."

"And did he say where he got the original to do the forgery?"

"From Rainey. Rainey's known for years who had it. He persuaded the guy to let Sorensen make a forgery for a share of the sale. Rainey brought both paintings to McCallister's, letting you do the authentication before making the switch. It was a good plan. If by any chance, a previous owner came forward to claim the painting, all they'd get was a forgery. Hutch is still trying to track down where the original is now."

"And who tipped off Philip Taurel that he'd bought the fake?"

"It was anonymous, so we'll probably never know, but it's likely Sorensen bragged about his work to someone."

"I still can't believe Walter Rainey would set me up like that. I thought he liked me." She snorted in disgust. "If it were John Allen, I could understand it."

"Yeah, well it's over now. Would you like to walk some more or find a coffee or soda or something? It's getting chilly, and you don't have a coat."

She stood, testing her shoes for comfort. "Walk, if that's okay."

He got to his feet and slipped his jacket off and put it around her shoulders. They wandered through to the garden's curved, wrought-iron pergola and leaned against the railing to look across the expanse of green, punctuated with summer color. She snuggled her face into the lapel of his jacket, savoring the familiar scent.

Suddenly, it was all clear to her. The past few weeks had been hell, but would she change a thing if it meant not having Mack in her life? Not for a minute. This incredibly sexy but vulnerable man was part of her life now.

"When do you go back?"

"Tonight."

She froze. "For how long?"

When he turned her face up to make sure she met his eyes, her pulse sped in fear.

"At least a year, maybe longer."

"Oh, God, no."

"Gemma, I can't make promises ... not in my world." He stepped forward and took her hands. "But I couldn't leave without seeing you."

He was telling her not to wait. "Is there any way I can contact you?" she asked hopelessly, barely able to force the words past her stiff lips.

"There's no contact allowed. It puts lives at risk."

"What can I do, Mack?"

He drew her to him as she closed her eyes, trying to trap the tears that spilled out over her cheeks down to her chin.

"Let me take a kiss, just like the one in the auction room."

By the time they'd drawn apart, it was drizzling again, mixing the raindrops with her tears.

CHAPTER SIXTEEN

One month later

"Isn't it beautiful?"

Mack rubbed the back of his neck, trying hard to look interested in yet another ceiling fresco. "Exactly what are we looking at, Dr. Gilmore?"

"You haven't listened to a word I've said, Mr. Buchanan," she sighed, letting the sound out slowly as if to emphasize her point. "This is the Museo Angelo fresco. The angels are exquisite, don't you think?"

"Uh-huh." He wasn't looking at the fresco. He was looking at Gemma, standing in a narrow shaft of sunlight streaming through an opening in the dome high above their heads. In her white dress, with her pale face framed by her long dark hair and staring upward, she looked like an angel herself.

"Started in 1642, finished in 1656."

"Did the guy get bored?"

"Philistine," she said with another sigh, her gaze still fixed to the ceiling.

"Yeah, and you wouldn't have me any other way."

"Don't be so sure."

He laughed. Yeah, he was sure. This was their first full day out of bed since their arrival in Venice. They'd still be in the sack if he hadn't felt guilty about her missing out on her frescos and statues and all the other art stuff she'd talked about on their flight two days ago.

This morning, he'd actually dragged the blankets off her and ordered her to get ready for a day's sightseeing. A damned

Herculean effort on his part, considering she was naked and kissing her way around his chest at the time.

She was still studying the angels, so Mack slipped his arms around her from behind, drawing her close.

"Where are the nudes?" he asked, nuzzling his mouth into the top of her head.

A woman's laugh tittered from somewhere behind them, and Gemma giggled. "You know she heard you. Everyone's looking."

"Uh-huh," he said, still nuzzling her hair. "What about we give them something to really look at?"

She turned inside his arms and smiled up at him, her glossy black hair shimmering in the soft sunlight. "You're hopeless. What would your boss say if he could see you now?"

"He'd say I was a lucky man."

"You still haven't told me how you wangled your way out of it."

Oh, she was about to get serious about that again. "That's classified. What's that thing over there?"

"Don't try and change the subject. How did you do it?"

He bent low, making her squirm when he blew warm air into her ear. "I said there was an incredibly talented, beautiful, persistent woman just begging for me to come home."

In fact, that's exactly what he'd said. Within twenty-four hours of reporting for duty, he'd made the decision to put in for more leave. But, under the unit's limited civilian contact rules, he hadn't been able to tell Gemma a thing about it. Besides, the odds of a 'yes' to his request were slim. The mission had been planned for over a year, and men with his particular set of skills were in short supply. But miraculously, it was granted, but only after an agonizing two-week wait for the decision. A whole six weeks to spend with her. And now, this morning ...

"I still don't believe you," she said into his thoughts. "You're not listening, are you?" She unwrapped herself from his arms to step back and study him. With her head cocked to one side and her hands on her hips, she looked like a very sweet, exasperated angel.

"I don't know what I'm going to do with you, Mack Buchanan."

Mack grinned, totally loving this whole flirting thing with her. "I can think of something." He went to snare her to him again, but she dodged his reach. "You've got a one-track mind." She pulled her guidebook from her bag and started flipping through the pages, pretending to be serious, but the corners of her mouth had curved high. "So what would you like to see now?"

There was only one answer to that question.

"Our hotel room."

"We can't. Not yet," she protested. He might have believed her if that betraying hitch in her voice hadn't told him she was seriously giving his suggestion some thought.

"Damn. Well, the next place better have nudes."

Mack took her hand and led her out of the Museo and down the steep steps to the piazza. Venice on a warm day. Tourists and sightseers crowded the square, chattering with excitement, posing for photos. In the past, he would have laughed at the thought of being part of this. He never could understand the whole tourism thing. But now he knew why people came to Venice.

Yeah, he'd gone soft. Hell, he wasn't the romantic type—at least not in the way women seemed to think of that kind of thing. But Venice on a summer's day, with Gemma beside him and the canals glittering under the late afternoon sun, had made him about as romantic as a man could get.

"You want a gelato?" she asked. She was looking at him with a small frown between her brows. "What are you thinking about?"

"You. I'll get the ice creams."

"In that case, stay where you are and think about me some more," she ordered with a laugh and disappeared into the gelateria beside the museum, emerging a minute later with two large strawberry ice creams.

They sat at a small outside table, licking their treats and watching the constant flow of sightseers strolling through the piazza beside the Grand Canal. He couldn't remember ever feeling so comfortable with someone or, for that matter, having so much fun. For the first time in years, he was utterly content. Enjoying Gemma's art chatter even though, most of the time, he barely knew what she talking about. Eating ice cream from a cone. Hell, he hadn't done that in years. It was fun. Gemma was fun. At first he'd imagined her to be one of those serious, arty types, but in the past weeks, he'd discovered how wrong he was. She made him laugh. Really laugh—that was something else he hadn't done in a long time. Then there was her incredible capacity for giving and taking pleasure.

"Omigosh! They've found the Bonvalet."

Mack blinked from his thoughts to see Gemma waving her phone at him.

"Wake up! John Allen says they found the Bonvalet in Atlanta."

"So the old boy came through." Recovering the painting and the money had always been a long shot. Their only hope had been to offer Rainey a generous plea bargain. Apparently, it had worked.

"He was due to retire next year," she said and he caught the sadness. "I know I shouldn't feel sorry for him after what he did to McCallister's. And me. But he was a nice man. Will he go to prison?"

Mack tossed his gelato cone in the trash and wiped his hands with a paper napkin. "Four years, max. He'll probably be out in two with good behavior. Watch it, you're about to drip on your dress."

"Oh hell." She licked her way up a trail of melted strawberry running down the cone.

Mack waited patiently until she'd finished her ice cream. He was a man on a mission, and he needed to get started. He got to his feet and rubbed his hands together. "On your feet, woman. Time to walk."

He sat back down, defeated, when she started thumbing through her phone again. She frowned. "McCallister's wants an answer by the end of the week."

"And?"

"I don't know."

Mack didn't press her. He knew she was still hurting over McCallister's' accusation. They'd hurt her badly, just like he had. He'd still not completely banished his guilt over not believing her. Perhaps he never would, but at least he'd learned to handle it now.

"Maybe I should accept the Enright offer." She began to chew at the corner of her mouth. One of her cute mannerisms that he now knew so well. "What do you think?"

"Have you thought of freelancing?" Not that he knew a thing about the art authentication business, but it seemed a reasonable option. "You are the best, apparently," he teased.

She pulled a face at him. "Actually, I could start my own business."

"Sounds like a plan. Actually, there's something I need to talk to you about ...." Mack stopped when a tourist group passed close to their table. Two elderly women straggling behind slowed when they spotted Mack. If the looks he was getting were anything to go by, that had to be the titterer and her friend from the Museo. He grinned at them, and they smiled back. He had the feeling he'd just made their day. Darned if he knew why.

Her head went to one side, her eyebrows up. "That sounds serious."

He stood and grabbed her hand, determined to get this done before he got interrupted again. "Let's walk."

He led her through the piazza and into one of the narrow winding streets that followed the Grand Canal. She was laughing at him, urging him to tell her where they were going, but he kept telling her to be patient. Trouble was, there was nowhere secluded enough for his purposes.

He was on the verge of giving up and taking her back to the hotel, when a small, secluded cobblestoned courtyard overlooking the canal opened up in front of his eyes. Perfect and, thank God, deserted.

Leading Gemma to the railing, he stopped and stood to collect his thoughts, aware that she was staring at him with a puzzled expression.

"What is it?" she asked, her voice now really serious. "Has something happened?"

He scratched his jaw, mentally rehearsing what he had to say.

"I've spoken to the agency about quitting for good." He paused when her mouth dropped open in surprise. "Anyway," he went on, "this morning, I got the approval."

"Oh."

Not much of a response, but he knew she was thinking hard about what that meant for him. For them. He'd already done his thinking. For weeks, he'd thought of nothing else but leaving the unit for good.

"So, here I am. Technically unemployed."

She tilted her chin up, searching his gaze. "Are you sure?"

"I'm sure." With her in his arms, he'd never been more sure of anything in his entire life.

"I love you, Gemma." His heart started to thump. He hadn't expected to feel so awkward. But then, this was a first for him. "I know it's been hell for you. I know you probably need time—"

"I love you, too."

Mack blinked. "Really?" Hearing her say the words was beyond any emotion he'd ever felt before, full of tenderness and sheer relief.

"Yes really," she confirmed, pressing her hand to his chest and smiling up at him. "I love you, Mack."

"Jesus," he muttered, then put a hand to his forehead. "Sorry, I'm an idiot."

Rising on her toes, she slipped her hands around his neck. "True. Now hurry up and kiss me."

When he finally let her up for air, she dropped back on her heels and tucked her face into his shirt. "I wish we didn't have to go home," she murmured.

"Would you come with me to Maine? I'll arrange for Tom and his family to be there so you can meet them." The sound of his chuckle brought her head up. "Man, will Tom be surprised. Big brother has finally fallen."

"I'd love to meet them." She smiled, looping her hands around his waist and snuggling into him again.

"It was a favorite place for Tom and me ... and my father.

He leaned down to her ear, his voice teasing. "So did your mother enjoy her latest cruise?"

She snorted before leaning back and rolling her eyes. "I guess. You know she'll blame you."

"What the hell have I done?"

"You're not Kyle. But don't feel bad. If I stubbed my toe, my mother would say it was because I didn't marry Kyle."

"I'll win her over," Mack answered with a grin. "After all, I saved her from having that jackass for a son-in-law."

Gemma shoved him back, laughing. "Don't talk about the jackass like that. He's a good man. No, really he is," she insisted, when Mack grimaced. "Besides, my mother only approves of filthy rich men."

"So, would moderately wealthy do?"

Mack laughed himself when she straightened, her mouth dropping open again. "What, *you*?"

"Don't look so surprised, my love." He shrugged. "All inherited from my mom's side. Her family never did get over her marrying an army major. Tom enjoys his wealth, but it's not really my thing."

"Well, don't tell my mother that. She'd think you were mad. But seriously, what will you do now?"

"Some consultancy work for the agency, probably training. The thing is," he said, fitting her hips to his, "I'm a man in love—useless as an operative now."

"No more Perses."

"Not true," he whispered into her hair. "I'm thinking of destroying our hotel bed, with you in it."

"But we haven't seen the Palazzo Campagna yet," she protested. "Surely, you wouldn't want to miss seeing that?"

"Are there any nudes?" he asked, earning him yet another one of her sighs.

"Not one. It's all landscapes."

"Then, Dr. Gilmore," he said quietly, his brows waggling wickedly and sending her into giggles, "it's the hotel for you."

"I guess the Palazzo will still be there tomorrow."

Mack leaned down and pressed a soft kiss to her mouth. "Yeah. And I'll get you there, even if it goddamn kills me."

"Okay, let's go home."

Mack smiled to himself as she hooked her arm through his and led him back into the street. It wouldn't matter where they went. He was already home.

About the Author

Susann Oriel lives in the Bay of Plenty, New Zealand. A love of books led her to become a librarian, later moving to the broader area of information management and technology—interesting, challenging, and fast-paced work in a rapidly changing environment. Then Susann discovered her inner romance writer. Now she's hooked on writing, and with the Bay's laid-back lifestyle and fabulous beaches on her doorstep, she has the perfect setting to create her stories.

A Sneak Peek from Crimson Romance
(From *The Arrangement* by Bethany-Kris)

A screech from Viviana's left side caused the pounding in her temple to increase.

"Vine, shut that damned thing off, would you?" Sam's husky voice reminded her of just who was in her bed and why she had yet to wake up. "You've hit the snooze a half a dozen times. Don't you have a lecture?"

Grumbling, she rubbed at her eyes. Finally, she blinked enough to feel awake and smacked at the alarm until it stopped beeping. Tossing blankets off the bed, her feet hit the cold floor. She barely recognized the time flashing on the alarm, but what her bleary eyes could see was enough to tell she was running late.

Really, really late.

"Why didn't you wake me up?" Viviana asked, scowling.

A tanned hand waved indifferently. Sam couldn't even be bothered to open his eyes and look at her. Some bodyguard he was.

"Like today is any different from yesterday?"

"This lecture is important!"

Clothes that had been carelessly scattered the night before were plucked up in her hands. Too much vodka and an attractive man made Viviana a messy girl. Eventually, she located the dark black skinny jeans and ribbed tank she'd worn the night before. Sniffing the clothes, they smelled decent enough, so she pulled them on and kicked around more stuff to find sneakers.

The sound of a glock's chamber being manually discharged stopped her heart for a split second. It brought back memories she'd buried deep in the depths of her mind. It was a sound she never wanted to hear again. The black jacket in her hands fell to the floor as she chanced a look over at the door, then to the window.

Instinct, that's what her father would have called it, because it was in her blood and bones. It didn't matter that she was a girl, and girls couldn't ever join the Cosa Nostra, she knew a fucking gun. Viviana could hold one, shoot like any made man, but that was only because her father said she had to learn.

The Don's child had to know how to shoot.

Dropping to all fours, she heard Sam laugh deeply.

"Chill, girl. I'm just checking the clip; my piece needs to be cleaned."

"I hate guns." Her voice was strained, anxiety eating away at her lungs that couldn't seem to inhale. "Put it away."

"Can't. I gotta check the floor before you go," he replied quietly. When Viviana's scowl made another appearance, he added, "Sorry. Those are the rules. You wanted freedom, so they gave it. I'm just one of the conditions that came along for the ride, babe."

A nauseous feeling settled in her like a heavy weight. "I've been here a year and there hasn't been an issue. Why can't you just leave?"

Sam swung his legs over the side of the bed, the movement drawing her eyes in to the bands of muscle that stretched and flexed all over his tanned form. The light dusting of hair that covered his chest and created a thin line to the spot between his legs had her memory on overload with images from the night before. He was all-American with a touch of Italian on the tip of his magic tongue. Kind of handsome. Cussed like a sailor, had a perfectly deadly sort of aim with a gun, and always stayed far enough away to never draw attention but close enough that she was still aware of his presence.

"You want me to leave after last night?"

Viviana refused to dignify that with a response. His cock stood at attention: hard, glorious, and probably still smelling like her pussy. Oh God, smelling like her. Panic saturated her from the inside out.

"Last night … tell me we used—"

"A condom," he interrupted. "Yeah. I don't fuck without one."

Sweet relief never felt so good. Sure, she was on the shot, but that didn't mean Sam wasn't out there fucking God knew who when he wasn't working.

Sam didn't pay Viviana's relieved sigh a moment of attention as he reached for his jeans. "I'll check the floors and you can go."

"What are we going to do?" she asked, shifting into a sitting position on the floor as he pulled on a pair of jeans. "Just … not tell anyone?"

Sam cringed. "That's probably best."

Probably, she thought sarcastically.

Being the daughter of a former mafia boss, Viviana should have known better. You didn't sleep with your bodyguard, and if they were worth anything, your bodyguard didn't make a move to bridge the personal gaps between you. Sam had been good, too. For the last year he'd done just what he needed, followed orders to the letter, and kept her as safe as he possibly could.

And then last night happened …

"Vine, you're freaking out over there when it's only me here. No one is gonna know we knocked boots if you don't say anything about it. I like my life right where it is, and I don't plan on swimming with the fish any time soon, so I sure as hell won't be saying a thing. If you want, I can request another man—"

"You're not made, right?"

Sam looked confused. "I'm not … *yet*."

She waved a hand between them. "Is this job your guarantee into it?"

The indignant sound he released was enough of an answer.

"It takes a little more than that, and you're not worth very much now."

"Well, great."

"No one likes to off a woman, Vine, especially if that woman is Roman's daughter. Doesn't matter if he's six feet under or not now, they already got your momma and brother. I suppose killing you just seemed cruel and unnecessary in the grand scheme of things. Be grateful they're letting you live."

"Grateful? They're just waiting for me to screw up and then …" Trailing off, Viviana made the shape of a gun with her thumb and forefinger and pulled the trigger at her temple. "*Boom*. I'll be the one swimming with the fish."

His unaffected, blank stare chilled.

"Your father might not be the boss now, but he was for a long time, and his daddy before him, too. Roman made a bad choice, so his men turned and did what they had to. Regardless, they'd show you more respect than an execution and a watery grave. You know that."

"A bad choice," Viviana repeated dully. That bad choice was her and a dozen other things that happened over two decades ago that she didn't want to think about. It was better if she didn't. There was less pain that way. "What the hell do you know about my father's *choices*? Just because those men spit what they call gospel doesn't mean they're not choking back on lies, Sam."

"Those *men* are *la famiglia*." Sam's warning rang loud and clear, causing Viviana to bite the inside of her cheek and look away. "As of today, they still consider you a part of that family. Gratitude and respect, Vine. Learn it."

"So says the man who fucked the *Don* of New York's daughter."

Sam grinned wickedly, pulling a V-neck T-shirt over his head. "Not the Don anymore. I was at the funeral, too. Besides, we can't do this again, right? I mean, you're a great lay, obviously, but I want my button and you're just a stepping stone to it."

"You can go to—"

"I'll make the call, Vine; get you another watcher. I'd rather be closer to New York, anyway. Sitting around in this place really isn't my thing. I know you're grieving, or whatever you want to call it, but it's been three years since your family was buried. Time to move on. It's not like some former mafia boss's daughter with no real connections can get her revenge, huh?"

Emotions betrayed Viviana by way of tears that welled up and threatened to fall.

"Fuck you, Sam."

"Already did, babe."

Standing to turn without another word, she slipped on the sneakers she managed to find under the corner chair before checking her face in the mirror. Red splotches had appeared on Viviana's cheeks from forcing back tears, lips still swollen from Sam's teeth biting and kissing the night before, and a small spot of red lipstick had smeared across the side of her mouth. Rubbing the stain with a makeup remover wipe from her dresser, she ran fingers through tangled waves of raven black hair as she tried to avoid the man's gaze behind her in the mirror.

"You know you're kind of beautiful, right?" Sam murmured behind her. His voice, thick with an Italian accent he could lay on heavy in a moment if he wanted, was rough and husky again. "They all say you look like your father, but you're a prettier version of your momma."

Brown eyes caught her own reflection in the mirror. What he said had some merit. With soft features, full lips, and wide eyes, Viviana certainly didn't go unnoticed by men. Regardless, she could pick out a dozen other parts of herself that she wasn't happy with. She hated the fact that her eyelashes weren't as long as her mother's once were, and that she mostly seemed to take after her in height, only standing a too-short five foot five inches.

Truthfully, Viviana didn't think she looked like her mother at all.

"We're not getting back into bed again, so you can stop it with your comments," she replied bitterly. Tilting her head to the side, the red mark he'd left on the spot between her shoulder and neck was on clear display. "I don't want your compliments."

Sam shrugged and dug through the mess on the floor to find his boots. "Just thought you should know, considering I didn't spend much time telling you last night. You're gonna make a man happy someday. The perfect little mob wife."

Leaning against the wall, he nodded at the calendar set up beside a small desk. "Your twenty-fifth birthday is coming up in three months, so when do you plan on settling down? God knows your uncle Sonny would love to see you married with a couple kids underfoot."

Shuddering at his words was the only indication she gave that she'd heard his statement. The uncle he spoke about was the same man who reportedly put a gun to her father's head and pulled the trigger. *Reportedly* because she knew it was truer than anyone else knew. He was also the man who took the throne of the Cosa Nostra within their family when her father was dead and gone. She had wondered later if Roman had seen Sonny coming, what with her uncle knowing of the deal her father had made with the Russians when she was only a toddler.

A snake, that's what her uncle was. A turncoat, untrue, traitor to her father and the family. His own brother marked the bullet and stained his hands a bloody red.

Blood didn't matter, though. Not in the family … or so Viviana had been told. Being a girl, it wasn't like she had been given the advantage of understanding the Cosa Nostra, its rules and values. In fact, just saying the word *mafia* or *mob* under her father's roof would get you one of his infamous looks, and then you knew you were in hot water.

The mafia doesn't exist.

Yeah, right.

Viviana's father had his own Wikipedia page, and her name was listed as his only surviving child right underneath.

"Don't talk about—"

The words were cut off by a loud bang. Once more, Viviana found herself on the floor, pushed there by Sam's hand.

Sam didn't join her on the floor; instead, she watched him reach for the glock twenty-two he'd tossed to the bedspread. That same gun he scared her with earlier, but forgot about in their argument. He never should have dropped his piece. The gun was his third hand, but she had made him forget about that important rule for a split second.

A split second too long.

The near silent pop, pop, pops—one right after the other—made her squeeze-shut her eyes and cover her ears. That only served to muffle the shouts from the attackers and her scream. Raw, achingly loud, and terrified, that's how her fear sounded. Something warm soaked into the side of Viviana's shirt. The heavy scent of gunpowder stung inside her lungs and she screamed again.

"Shut her up!"

The voice was bottomless, scratchy with age, and thick with an accent that made a cold shiver of dread roll through Viviana's body. She hadn't heard a Russian drawl in years. It was the last thing she expected to encounter again, given they hadn't come for her after her family's murder.

"No!"

Viviana kicked out, turning to the side and stumbling over a mess on the floor. Reaching for the cell phone right beside the bed, she felt hands grabbing at her legs, pulling roughly and dragging her away from potential salvation.

If she could have reached the phone … maybe … maybe she … Viviana was alone.

No one's daughter anymore.

The mafia princess without a crown.

"Don't touch me! *Sam*!"

The first man inside the doorway spoke, his words switching from English to Russian. Whatever he said, the man still pulling Viviana towards him as she kicked out and punched at him only grunted back in response. When her small fist landed a solid smack to his nose, his blue eyes narrowed before he shouted something she couldn't understand. He raised his large hand and hit her sharply on the cheek. It bloomed with instant pain. Air sucked into her frozen lungs; she was shocked and speechless that a man had hit her.

The man shouted again, and even in Russian, his warning was clear. Viviana watched stunned as the butt of a gun snapped down with a loud smack to his comrade's head.

"Fool, you're not to hurt her! He will have your life for that. Move, Viktor."

"Don't touch me," she hissed. Deciding fighting wasn't going to help her when he bared his teeth and spit more words she couldn't understand, Viviana exposed her own teeth in a last ditch effort to rebel. "Keep your filthy fucking hands off of me, scum."

"I said move. We need to leave." In a flash, the man named Viktor was pushed off Viviana, and someone else clouded her blurring vision. Hot tears fell as Viviana stared up with her lips trembling, hair stuck to a damp face, and the taste of blood saturating her mouth. "I am Boris, girl. Up with you, before some other drunk college student wakes and calls the police."

Both men wore flat black from head to toe, their hair slicked back making them look odd and startling. She guessed their ages to be late thirties to early forties, and by the job they had been sent to do, it wouldn't have surprised Viviana if they were only bulls for the Russian mafia. Bulls being a term the Bratva used to describe their bodyguards, as the men were often large, frightening, and known for their violent tendencies.

"S-Sam ... he—"

"Dead," Boris replied in a cold and distant tone, eyes flickering up to look behind Viviana's prone body. It wasn't a second later before he was bending down and grabbing at her wrists to pull her up to unsteady feet. "Do not act so shocked, Miss Carducci. You've witnessed death in one form or another. He is but a snail in comparison to the rest of the world you live in."

"I don't live in that world anymore."

Viviana glanced pointedly around her messy dorm room. There were scattered papers on the desk and mismatched photos and mementos attached to the wall to hide the cracking paint. The room was as messy as a pigsty. Did she look like she was living her spoiled lifestyle as a mafia child? Wasn't it obvious she'd already cut her ties, or tried to?

"I'm a student, not a Don's daughter."

The words seemed to go unheard, as Boris pushed her at Viktor, who openly glared. Blood dripped down his nose to cover his scowling lips. A strange sense of satisfaction filled Viviana at the sight.

"Why are you here?"

Boris sighed as he opened the drawers to the dresser and pulled out a hoodie and other articles of clothing. The items were tossed into a pile on the floor.

"Your purse, where is it?"

"Why are you here?" Viviana repeated.

Viktor's hand stuck out again, fingers painfully gripping her jaw as he shook her face and snarled, "I've had just about enough of your nonsense, you little bitch. Now, answer his question!"

Her heart thudded louder, pushing out an achingly hard and fast beat. "On the hook behind the door." Suddenly, Viviana didn't feel so courageous. She attempted to hold back tears. "I don't have money; Uncle Sonny doesn't give—"

"I want to ensure you have a passport," Boris interrupted, turning to half close the door they'd kicked open to find her purse.

The contents scattered across the cheap, worn carpet. "Canada was not a safe place for you, and now we're taking you back. You have a deal to uphold. That is why we are here."

"My father is dead; that deal is void."

Viktor's narrowed eyes turned on Viviana in anger and she instantly flinched away. The last thing she wanted was him hitting her again. Viktor smiled, the sight causing her stomach to roll; blood covered his teeth, turning them garish and disgusting.

"Deals with the dead are still upheld in the Bratva, girl. Their family upholds it personally. We make sure of that."

"By twenty-five, it was agreed," Boris said. "You were to be married, like it or not." With a jerk of his head, Viktor released her face. Exhaling shakily, she forced herself not to rub her aching jaw. "You're three months off from that date, so my Pakhan is requesting your presence."

"*Pah … kun.*" Given the answering frown from Boris, Viviana knew her attempt at the Russian word was poor at best. "What is that?"

"Who," he corrected with a small smile. "The boss. You call them the Don or Boss, but we Russians call them Pakhan. Or Boss, depending on his mood. Nicoli—"

"Is dead, just like my father. So their deals should be, too."

"Stop arguing, it's done!" Boris snapped.

What she knew of the Russian mafia was very little, and the information she had gained over the years were from discussions she hadn't been meant to hear. Any interest Viviana outwardly showed for the Bratva—a family so similar to her own—after her father's death was brushed off with a warning about loyalty and blood. She just wanted to understand why they'd done what they did by arranging the marriage between her and the grandson of a Bratva boss.

"Who requested me?"

The question came out strained, sounding almost foreign. Weak and scared, that's what they made her. She was a boss's daughter—a mafia child. Never should she be feeble and pathetic. Still, Viviana was confused. Knowing they had several upper bosses, and given the structure in their business, well, it wasn't something she considered organized, so she had to know for sure who was requesting her.

"Who wants me, now?"

"You know who."

"No, I don't."

Boris checked his watch. "We don't have time for this. The border is a—"

"Who?" Viviana forced out.

"Anton."

Her shoulders slumped, confusion and fear rising in a mere breath of air. Anton Avdonin was the other half of the deal made between men who no longer lived. Anton, a man two years and two months older than she was, a full-blooded Russian who she only met twice in her life. He was also the grandson of a formally notorious mob boss in the Russian mafia, also known as the Bratva. Situated largely in Brighton Beach, New York, the Bratva was known to meddle in guns and narcotics trafficking, as well as money laundering and prostitution.

Viviana had a lot in common with Anton in some aspects. She was, after all, the daughter of one of the world's most dangerous Cosa Nostra Dons. Italian in bloodline, the Cosa Nostra started as a Sicilian-based mafia who considered their unit a family structure. They, too, handled running guns and drugs, as well as partaking in other illegal operations to make money.

Why, she wondered. Why now, when he could move on, forget about it, and take whoever else he wanted for a wife? Surely after nine years, whatever connection she thought they had was all but gone, right?

"But, he *can't*."

Boris eyed her like Viviana had grown a second head. Despite the situation, her nerves were making an appearance by way of the inappropriate laughter that bubbled its way out from her chest into dead air.

"He can. Anton is preserving the wishes of his dead grandfather and your father. It was important to him."

"But I'm useless!" she cried, feeling tears well and fall again. "Nothing to him—not Russian, not connected, and just … a *fucking liability*."

With a sharp whisper in Russian, Boris grabbed her roughly and forced Viviana to move. The long barrel of a silencer pressed to her side. "Now, shut those lips of yours, Miss Carducci. We wouldn't want to wake up the rest of this dorm and cause more issues than necessary. A car is waiting for us at the entrance. Viktor will meet us five miles past the border after he cleans up."

Only then did she notice the plastic gas cans sitting outside in the hallway. Even though it was late afternoon and the hallways were seemingly quiet, there were still students and faculty in the building. "You can't burn—"

"I will tape your mouth shut, girl, if you can't keep quiet. I promise."

As he dragged Viviana from the room, she made the mistake of looking back.

Sam's still form was sprawled half on, half off the bed. Struck helpless, he was far too pale to be alive. Blood and matter had splattered across the wall behind him. Open, dead eyes stared blankly as blood ran red with spidery lines over the muscles on his arm, slipping in slow dribbles from his fingers to soak into the floor.

The vomit she had been holding back finally made its way out.

In the mood for more Crimson Romance?
Check out *Blitzkrieg Love* by Livia Olteano
at *CrimsonRomance.com.*

www.ingramcontent.com/pod-product-compliance
Lightning Source LLC
Chambersburg PA
CBHW010309100726

47905CB00011B/3277